THE TEQUILA

A KILLERS NOVELLA

BRYNNE ASHER

THE TEQUILA

A Killers Novella
Brynne Asher

Published by Brynne Asher
BrynneAsherBooks@gmail.com

Keep up with me on Facebook for news and upcoming
books
https://www.facebook.com/BrynneAsherAuthor

Join my Facebook reader group to keep up with my latest
news Brynne Asher's Beauties

Keep up with all Brynne Asher books and news. Sign up
for my newsletter http://eepurl.com/gFVMUP

Edited by Hadley Finn
Cover by Haya in Designs

CONTENTS

ALSO BY BRYNNE ASHER

To Ty,
May you never know anything other than love and family.
xoxo

1

HANGOVER

Mary

I'M GOOD. I really am. I mean, it took me almost forever, but I'm finally handling life like a C-list rock star. You know, the one who opens for the opener of the main act? The one nobody's heard of but they've made a little something of themselves?

Yeah, I'm pretty sure I finally made it to that level in life. I mean, I can't say I'm great but, since there were times when I was really not great, I can, with all honesty and confidence, say I'm good.

Until him.

Until the wine.

And, strap me up and take away my deep-conditioning hair mask, until the *tequila*.

The tequila is what did me in.

What was I thinking?

So, I might've had some wine to take the edge off. But I needed it.

I don't know why I thought it would be a good idea to

chase the wine with tequila. We were at an Italian restaurant for God's sake.

But I did. And I drank *all* the tequila.

Then I drank some more and thought the tequila
needed dessert. So, of course, in my freak-out moment, I
decided that topping off the tequila with tiramisu was the
best thing since dipped nails.

All because of him. No one's ever made me nervous,
wet, agitated, and hardened my nipples all at the same
time.

But when I woke up this morning in a strange bed—a
bed in a bedroom I'd never seen before—every distilled
drop of blue agave turned in my stomach like a bad decision on spring break at the beach.

I only experienced one spring break—college was
torture and sucked my joy. Secondary education and I got
along like my second, fifth, and sixth sets of foster parents
—if you could call them that. There wasn't much
parenting going on and living in those houses was like
trying to survive a constant bar brawl. I dropped out of
college shortly into my second year and enrolled in
cosmetology school the same day.

When I spin my clients around in the chair and see
their smile in the mirror, I know I made the right choice.
Making people feel good about themselves is the best part
of my job. I love hair, nails, color, and everything girlie.
My penchant for pretty things leans toward edgy with a
hint of glam.

I switch up my locks regularly. My long, naturally
blond hair is always dyed to match the water-colored ink
crawling up the small of my back. Give me a client who's
willing to push the envelope and I'm in hairdresser

heaven. Secretly, I've always found anything conventional and conservative boring as hell.

That was, until *him*.

Evan Charles Hargrove III.

He's more all-American than the boy next door, the Fourth of July, and red Solo cups all rolled into one. He might look like a frat boy with his tall, muscular frame and rugged good looks, but he's the tasting room manager at Whitetail Farms. Evan knows more about wine than ninety-nine percent of the population. If I wanted to eat Twizzlers and dark chocolate for dinner—which I do on the regular—he'd pair it perfectly and seduce me while doing so.

His hair is a little overgrown but fits him so perfectly, it makes me want to wash it, run my fingers through it, and style it into the messy do he wears so well. That, along with his whiskey eyes, perfect jawline, and self-confidence of a Fortune 500 CEO, makes him the kind of guy I'll cross the street and walk an extra three blocks out of my way to avoid.

That's why I'm always shocked and amazed whenever his gaze settles on me and I find myself weak in the knees and wet in my personal paradise.

That is, when he's not pissing me off. And, oh, how he loves to piss me off.

If he's not calling me *mermaid girl*, he's teasing me for being short. When he's not teasing me, he's complaining how I never take his appointment when he calls the shop to schedule a haircut.

I've cancelled his appointment five times because I don't think I could handle having him in my chair, let alone touching him. I'd end up strangling him or having a mini-orgasm and either would be bad for business.

But Evan works for my best friend, Addy Wentworth. Addy has a way of collecting people and if you're in her life, you're her friend *for* life, so that means Evan is my friend even though he's the one person I've made it my number one goal to avoid.

He's my frenemy.

I think he knows it, too, as I've done my best to ignore him. But somehow, my best is never quite good enough. When it comes to him, I turn foggy and weak.

I see it in every lethal look hidden behind his boy-next-door good looks. When he calls me a fairy—for being small and colorful—and if no one's looking, he'll tip his head and wet his lips with the tip of his tongue, making me wonder if he's thinking about what else he can do with it. I sure as hell am.

Don't even get me started on all the ways he finds to secretly touch me when no one's paying attention—brushing the small of my back or letting his fingertips lightly tease mine in erotic foreplay. It drives me mad in a multitude of ways.

But the other day—the moment my past came crashing into my present—he caught me off guard and broke through my defenses, informing me he was taking me to dinner. I was shaken by a text I'd just received from my childhood friend, Piper, and distractedly tried to refuse. But with the finesse of a corporate giant closing the deal of the decade, he shook his head and squashed my denial like a bug. I swear, he saw the crack in my armor and took advantage. "I'm taking you to Girasol's. You love Italian and I'm trying to sell them on adding The Delaney on their wine list."

The Delaney is Addy's red blend, named after her mom, and, since Addy is one of my best friends, I couldn't exactly refuse him for the sake of friendship and all that loyalty jazz. Like the three idiots we turn into around this undercover sexy-beast, my nipples and I were speechless and had no choice but to pucker and nod.

Since I was wound tight about the possibility of my worlds colliding—the one I hate more than anything and the one I've come to love more than life itself—I thought a little drink to loosen me up wouldn't hurt. Downing a half-bottle of Meritage was my pre-date coping mechanism.

Then I started in on the tequila.

All. Of. It.

Okay, fine. Maybe not *all* of it.

But I don't recall leaving the restaurant so there was no chance of remembering anything after that. It turns out, Evan brought me back to his condo, put me in his bed, and I woke up in my clothes from last night.

That's how I earned this hangover that's stewing while Evan drives me back to my car at the winery where we met before dinner.

I've decided to title this latest chapter of my life from hell *The Ride of Shame*.

My outfit is rumpled. I have raccoon eyes. My head is pounding and my stomach is churning like the butter from my *Little House on the Prairie* books. But thanks to my T-3 curling iron, my hair is still leaning on the side of fabulous.

With my shoes dangling from a finger, I drag my ass and try to pretend I'm human, crawling out of Evan's car as he follows.

He's tall, towering over me, and I'm reminded of all the times he's called me *shortie*. Leaning in, he puts his lips to my ear. "Fun night. Just so you know, we're doing it again soon but you're not drinking a drop of liquor, my little dandelion."

Little dandelion?

Oh, fuck.

He knows about my obsession for the pesky weed most people work hard to abolish from their little corner of the earth. This isn't good. What else did I blab about last night?

I squint into the sun when his hand cups my chin and tips my head back and he narrows his eyes on me. "And that little issue you told me about? I want to know more about that, too."

Shiiiiiit.

What have I done?

I open my mouth to argue because there are so many reasons I don't need Evan in my life right now—the top two of those being I've been hit by a freight train in a tequila bottle and him butting into my latest drama will certainly taint his perfect, red-Solo-cup life.

From here on out, my number one goal is to avoid Evan Hargrove.

But his thumb stops me with a brush of my lips, effectively shutting me up. "No arguments. Go drink lots of water or, if you have any, Gatorade. Pedialyte is even better. Then eat something and go back to bed. I'll stop by later to check on you. And Mary," he leans in farther and presses his lips to the skin just below my ear, making my already-wobbly knees about to give and make me expire like the heroines from my bodice-ripper romances, "thanks for a fun night. I thought I wanted you before, but now? I can't wait to make you mine. Be prepared."

Prepared? I'm not even prepared for last week.

With that, he doesn't give me a chance to respond. He

gives me that look that holds the secrets I'm afraid to learn before turning back to his car.

Shit, shit, *shit*. Evan was already obnoxiously persistent. And since I can't remember anything past the bruschetta, it turns my stomach in new ways to think about what upped his relentlessness to new heights.

The bright morning sun is making it hard to think, so I do the only thing I can manage at the moment. With my racoon makeup, pounding head, and fabulous hair, I dig my keys out of my bag and fall into my driver's seat. I need a shower, my bed, and to call Piper to find out what in the living hell is going on in Massachusetts.

2

CALM YOUR TITS

Mary

I GULP DOWN three Advil and check my phone. Two calls and a slew of texts from Piper last night during my drunken state, along with another voicemail from some guy in New York I do not know and I'm not about to call back, has me wanting to bury myself in a hole never to see daylight again. I know I should be a responsible adult and at least return Piper's call, even though I'd rather give a pedicure to an ogre than face what's going on in Massachusetts.

What's another fifteen minutes?

I drag myself into the shower and hope the hot water will make me feel human.

It doesn't work.

My phone vibrates on the bathroom counter as I'm drying off and I'm not surprised when I see who it is.

Clutching my towel to my chest, I greet my childhood friend. "I know you miss me but this is borderline stalker behavior. I'm thinking about a restraining order."

"Mary, I swear, if you didn't live hours away from me, I'd be knocking down your door right now. Where have you been?"

I drop my towel and grab my silk kimono robe off the back of my bathroom door, doing my best to shrug it on as I cringe, admitting to my childhood friend that I finally caved to Evan's annoying-yet-sexy advances. "I went on a date."

I get nothing but silence, which doesn't surprise me because I don't date and since Piper knows absolutely everything there is to know about me, I bet she's more surprised about it than I am.

I sigh. "I know, I know. I went on a date. If you're gonna go drama queen on me, would you just get it over with? I have a hangover."

"You went on a *date*?" she echoes. "With who? And if you tell me you're dating your old tattoo artist again, I really will drive to Virginia and shake some sense into you. He's an ass and doesn't deserve to share your oxygen. Wait—scratch that. He doesn't deserve oxygen. That pile of shit has earned carbon dioxide for what he did to you—"

"Piper!" I wince as my voice pin-balls around my head and move to my room to collapse onto my messy, unmade bed. "Calm your tits. It wasn't him."

"Oh." I hear men talking in the background and realize she's at work. Piper owns her own bakery, and she just got married, too.

When it comes to adulting, Piper is killing it.

"Then who is it? Anyone I know?" she goes on.

I pull my pillow to my chest and shut my eyes. "You don't know anyone since you've never come to Virginia to visit me."

Her voice turns muffled. "Can you get the cookies out of the oven, please. I'll be back in three minutes." She turns her attention back to me. "I don't have time for the guilt trip, I have customers lined out the door. You can tell me all about your date later when you *call me back*," I almost hear her roll her eyes, "but for now, I have news. Jake's friend called me last night with new information."

I groan and pull the pillow over my head to hide from daylight and life in general.

"Girl." The background has gone quiet so I assume she's moved into her office for some privacy and she softens her voice, like that's going to make whatever she's about to tell me go down easier. "The rumors are true. Your dad is back and was spotted at a bar across town."

I squeeze my eyes shut. "I guess hoping he was somewhere dead was too much to ask for, huh?"

"I told Jake about him and he spread the word. Trust me, between my husband, his friends, we've got a pulse on what's going on."

I pry my eyes open and look across my small bedroom at my garage sale furniture littered with empty Diet Coke cans. "And did they hear anything?"

After a long pause—one that's heavy and filled with unease, making my stomach turn in a whole other way—she gives it to me straight. "He's looking for you. Asking anyone and everyone he comes into contact with. One of Jake's friends overheard. Your father is relentless."

I roll to my back and stare at the stained ceiling of my crappy apartment. "He'll find me. From everything I know about him, I know he will."

"I know this sounds crazy since your dad is here, but what do you think about coming home? I worry about you all the way in Virginia by yourself. You could stay with

Jake and me or with my dad. There's no way Duane Giesen would get near you."

I've always been alone. Sure, I have friends, clients, and clients who have become friends. Hell, Addy has practically adopted me as a little sister and I've gladly allowed it. I love her and the small fold she's brought me into at the winery. But Piper is right. I am alone because there's no way I'm admitting to anyone here about the life I left behind in Boston.

That still doesn't mean I can pick up and leave. "I have to work. I can barely take a vacation for fear my clients will find someone new to make them beautiful. As tempting as that sounds, picking up and hiding out in Massachusetts isn't an option. I just don't understand ... after all these years, why he's looking for me now?"

She sighs. "I knew you were going to say that and I don't understand, either. None of us can figure out what he wants."

The pounding in my head won't stop, especially now that I not only have to worry about Evan, but also my damn father who's never acted like one a day in his life. "You have customers to tend to and I need a nap. I'll be fine. Let me know if he skips town and I'll jump into the Potomac and freestyle it downstream. He never learned how to swim unless he took lessons in prison."

"You're crazy, Mary."

I close my eyes and mumble, "Given the humans who made me, this surprises you?"

She ignores that, probably because she knows it's the truth. "I'll keep you up to date on what's going on here but, dammit, answer your phone."

"I promise."

"Sleep off your hangover so you can make the world beautiful."

I yawn. "Deal."

"Deal."

Piper hangs up, but not before I hear her greet a customer who orders an insane amount of cupcakes.

3

BROKEN

Evan

I STARTED WORKING at the vineyard when I was in college. I didn't need a job but was bored out of my mind. Per my dad's demands, I got a degree in business even though I never wanted to work in an office. I also never gave a shit about wine until I got a job here and was basically a catch-all, part-time employee to help out the property caretaker, Morris. I worked in the fields, watched the grapes grow, took part in harvest, and Van taught me about fermentation.

What I did not do was go to work for my family, who has been in the horse breeding business for generations. That irritated my dad, but since he'll do anything to make my mom happy and she didn't give a shit, he got over it. I finished college, not because I was learning anything practical, but because I knew someone with a big stick up their ass would someday value me more because I have a piece of paper in a leather binder stuffed away somewhere in my old room at my parents' house as proof that they overpaid for a degree at a private university.

Since then, I worked my way into the tasting room. The last owner was a dumbass and caused a lot of people to quit, so I was promoted to the tasting room manager— for no other reason than there were no other choices. That was right before Addy bought the place. I've seen the vineyard change hands three times, but all the owners were hobbyists who thought a winery would be a pretty accessory in their portfolio. That is, until they lost money hand over fist. That's never a fun hobby.

But the new owner, Addy Wentworth, actually has more brains than money and has turned the place around. We're making more than we're spending, which is a modern miracle. Everyone is happy about it because Addy is cool as shit to work for and making money means we get to keep our jobs.

Working here is more fun than working for my name-sake, so I decided to learn wine and it stuck. I like the people here and, even though it doesn't pay what my father would if I were managing his breeding business, it's a good place to be. I don't need the money anyway. I have a trust from my grandparents that I've never even touched.

The winery has been an even better place to be since Mary started coming around. Addy claims people as her own—hell, I'm one of them. Since the day she took over, our odd-as-hell group has become a close-knit clan that would rival any weird holiday movie.

"I've been waiting for you. How did it go?"

Speak of my boss, she's stalking straight for me in a way that has nothing to do with wine. I shrug off my jacket and toss it onto the bar. Pushing my hand through my hair, I try not to think about watching Mary sleep in my bed last night because I have no desire to have to hide my hard-on in front of my boss. "Last night? My steak was good."

Her eyes go big. "You know what I mean."

I turn away from her and start to dig through my bag for my tablet. "You should ask your friend."

"I tried!" Addy is edging on desperate which is odd for her since she usually has her shit together. But her new neighbor, Crew Vega, has been hanging around and she seems off her game. "Mary's not answering my calls and I know her car was parked here all night."

I turn back to her and shake my head. "She had a lot to drink and couldn't drive home."

Addy processes that for a hot second before throwing her next words at me in a way she's never done before. "Where did you take her?"

I consider Addy a friend and I'm pretty sure she considers me something like a younger brother. Even so, I know for a fact she and Mary are tight and based on girl code alone, she'd fall on the side of Mary every time, should there ever be sides to fall on, even though I don't plan on that happening. Still, I don't like her tone and frown. "You think I'm that kind of asshole?"

Her expression blanks and, when her hands hit her hips, her eyes narrow. "You know I don't think you're an asshole. Mary and I are tight. Besides all of you here at work, she's the best friend I have in Virginia. As close as we are, I know there are things she holds back from me. If you plan to pursue her, you have to promise it's because you want more than a fling. She might come off as tough as nails but she's not. Don't ask me how I know this, I just do. I *feel* it."

My guess? Addy doesn't have a clue how close she is to the truth.

Mary has done her best to avoid me, which has only piqued my interest. She's been dancing around me with nervous energy, pretending she hates me and doesn't have a bit of interest. Even though last night didn't go as I planned, it couldn't have gone any better because she let loose. The sexual tension I know I've felt all this time is there—it's real, tangible, and, once she let the tequila settle into her bones, the words flowed straight from her soul.

I still don't know everything about her, but I know a hell of a lot more than I did yesterday at this time.

I thought I wanted her before last night.

I had no fucking clue.

But today? Today, I need her in a way I can feel in every cell of my body. The petite girl with the mermaid hair who used to make me smile, now makes me ache.

I look to my boss and tell her the cold, hard truth. "I learned a lot last night and all I'm going to say is you've never been more right. She's not tough as nails and she's not fragile—she's broken."

Addy's face falls.

"Yeah," I confirm the thoughts written all over her face. I take my tablet and grab my jacket, leaving her with a promise before I head to the office in the back room. "But I'm going to be the one who helps put her back together. Starting today."

"Evan?" I'm almost out the door and cringe when Addy calls for me again. I'm not in the mood to have my motives questioned.

I sigh and look back one more time. "Yeah?"

In the time I've worked for her, I've never seen Addy

more serious and that's saying something because she's a smart and shrewd business woman. "Do whatever you have to do and don't give up. She doesn't know it but she needs you. Promise me you'll put her back together and do it with care."

That's an obligation I have no trouble keeping. "I promise."

The last thing I see before turning to my office is a sad smile settle onto my boss's face. I have some calls to make this morning before I start fulfilling that promise sooner rather than later.

Checking up on Mary's hangover is a perfect place to start.

4

CHERRY STEMS AND LIES

Mary

OH FUCK, THE banging.

It needs to stop.

The midday sun breaks through my lids and I realize the hammering isn't coming from inside my head. Someone's beating on my door. I pick up my cell that's lying on the bed next to me from where it fell from my sleepy grip when I hung up with Piper and see it's only a little after one o'clock.

I crawl out of bed and shuffle my way through my apartment as the incessant banging continues. Cinching my kimono robe tight, I throw the lock and open the door without checking to see who it is, if for no other reason than to stop the noise.

The smell hits me first—something greasy and probably from a drive-thru—before I look up and see Evan. After all I put it through last night, my stomach doesn't turn at the succulent scent of fried food, but instead grumbles. When I look down, he's holding a huge bag in one hand and a fountain drink in the other, causing my mouth to go dry. If that's a cheeseburger and Diet Coke, I might fall to my knees and weep.

"Thought I'd take my lunch hour to check on you and make sure you fed that hangover, but I've gotta say, the way you're lusting after this burger and fries makes me jealous."

My eyes jump to his that are hiding behind a pair of Ray-Bans and it's only from the tilt of his head that I can tell his eyes have dropped to my body.

"We need to talk about last night," he adds.

I lean onto the door and wonder what he'd do if I grabbed the food and slammed the door in his face? I'm starving and don't want to talk—desperate times call for desperate measures. "We can talk another time, like in a few months at Addy's Christmas party. I'm sure you have to get back to the tasting room. I hear Monday afternoons are busy."

His lips tip on one side because he knows I'm full of shit. The tasting room is closed on Mondays and I'm surprised he was even at work.

He has the audacity to lift my drink that he's still holding to his lips and take a pull from the straw as he flicks his shades off. I frown as he teases me with my post-hangover drug. "You know we're closed today, even though I'd risk Addy firing me for you. There are things I want to know and you're not getting one french fry until you let me in."

My stomach growls and he hears it too because his smirk turns into a smile.

"You talking is a small price to pay for greasy drive-thru to settle your stomach," he adds.

My brow quirks. "It's rude to talk with your mouth full."

"Yeah?" His eyes rake down to my turquoise painted toes one more time before boomeranging back to mine and this time his are intense. "Who taught you that?"

I nibble on the side of my lip. With the hints he gave me this morning of our date last night, I have a feeling that question holds more weight than its face value. "I learned it while watching reruns of *The Brady Bunch* on Nick at Nite. Alice was a stickler for table manners."

He shakes his head and, transferring the greasy sack to his hand holding my drink, opens it. Without taking his eyes off mine, he reaches in and produces a french fry, tossing it between his full lips, speaking with his mouth full. "I've never watched The Brady Bunch. You've gotta let me in if you're hungry, otherwise I'm gonna stand out here and eat it all in front of you."

"Is there cheese on that burger?"

He licks the salt off his fingers. "Yeah. It's a double."

I lick my lips.

What the hell? I need that burger.

I start to open my door all the way for him and, just when I am about to ask if he brought me my favorite fountain drink, he moves, forcing me to step back and trip over the shoes I tossed when I got home this morning. He kicks the door shut with his boot and doesn't stop.

"What are you doing?" I ask, still moving backward as he advances on me.

I barely have the chance to sidestep him as he strides toward my kitchen. "You're going to eat and answer my questions."

I follow, watching him fill my space. My apartment is

small and dingy and I could afford so much more, but why? It's just me and I'm fine right here.

But I have this man in my home—a man I've had to pretend doesn't make me nervous. Evan makes my space seem miniscule.

I tug on my robe to tighten it and watch him drop his sunglasses, food, and, what I pray is a Diet Coke, on the counter.

I open the bag and pull out two fries. They practically melt in my mouth they taste so good.

Evan crosses his arms across his wide chest and leans his hip into the counter, facing me, as I start to dig into the bag.

"Why did you move to Virginia by yourself when you were eighteen?"

My jaw freezes mid-chew. That's not what I expected him to ask, but it is telling as to what I blabbed about last night in my drunken state along with my obsession for pesky flowers.

I swallow. "See? You think you know so much, but the joke's on you. I was eighteen and a half."

He tips his head. "You're not nearly as funny now as you are when you're drunk."

I shrug and keep feeding my hangover. The greasy fries are a balm to my queasy stomach. "I don't tie one on very often, so there's no reason for you to stick around and experience me sober." I raise my hand with salt-covered fingers. "Boring to the bone."

He ignores me. "Why did you move to the middle-of-nowhere, bum-fuck Virginia?"

I reach in the sack again. "I came for George Washington and I stay for the free wine and cows that come with being Addy's friend."

He narrows his eyes. "Who kept calling you last night? You had more calls and texts than most people get in a week and, every time I asked, you grumbled some mumbo-jumbo about your past life coming back to bite you in your sweet ass."

With that, my stomach isn't grumbling anymore. It's clenching and twisting.

He lowers his voice and takes a step. I have to tip my head to look up at him, he's so much taller than me standing on bare feet. "Unless you're a time-traveler, I want to know about this past life of yours because I don't plan on anyone getting close to your ass besides me."

I swallow hard and shift my weight. Feeling the heat radiating from him, along with talk of him anywhere near my ass, causes me to become wet where I'm pantyless.

He reaches up and twirls one of my long curls around his index finger as his eyes wander over me. "I promise I won't bite it."

I rub my thighs together and squeeze my eyes shut. "Evan, please."

He doesn't stop. "Okay, if you're into that, I have no problem biting you."

My eyes fly open and the next thing I know, his single finger curled around my teal-colored hair turns into a fist. "I guess I'll just have to kiss it out of you."

Then his hand grips the back of my neck and his lips land on mine.

It's such a shock, my breath catches and my lips part.

For the first time ever, I'm kissing Evan Charles Hargrove III. I'm so glad I brushed my teeth earlier.

I mean, I've had my share of first kisses and this is *not* your run-of-the-mill encounter with another set of lips.

His mouth devours mine as he turns and presses me

into the counter, our bodies making full-on contact. I feel every one of his toned muscles press into my small, soft curves through my thin robe. That tongue, which has teased me so many times when he's sent me secret looks, plunges into my mouth as desperate as a starved sailor abandoned at sea. With one hand in my hair and the other reaching down to fist my kimono at my thigh, he's everywhere, making my heart speed.

I've tried not to dream of Evan, but I'm weak and not disciplined in much of anything. It doesn't matter how much I've tried to avoid his attention because we just don't fit, this kiss is everything I imagined it would be.

Yet, so much more.

Dragging his hand up my body, the silk pulls with his touch and he brushes the bottom of my breast through the thin material. I can't help it—I moan against his tongue as it explores me. This spurs him on and he deepens his kiss. His big hand cups my breast and squeezes, roughly pinching my nipple between his index finger and thumb.

The sensation shoots straight south and I gasp for air. "Evan."

He pulls his head back, his chest rising and falling—just as affected by our first kiss—and stares into me. "You said so many things last night, I don't even know where to start with you."

I frown and try to catch my breath, but he still has a firm hold of my breast and isn't letting go. I swallow and try to fidget but he presses his hips into me. His cock, thick and hard, indents my belly, making me wetter than I already was. "I was drunk. I can't be held responsible for what I say under the influence."

He hikes a brow. "People are honest when they're drunk."

"Not me," I lie, now more worried than ever about how I can recover from my drunken prattling. "I'm a big, fat liar when I drink. I'm famous for it. It's my signature party trick."

His lips tip and suddenly those perfect all-American white teeth glint at me. "Party trick?"

"Yeah. Everyone has one. Like tying a cherry stem into a knot with my tongue. Cherry stems and lies. I'm known for them."

His voice dips and he pinches my nipple again, twisting this time. "Maybe you'd like to talk more about what you can do with your tongue."

I give my head a shake but more to ward off the shiver running down my spine from what he's doing to my breast rather than his words. "No. I don't think that would be a good idea, either."

He gives me another squeeze and my body heats—the silk like wool on a hot summer day. "Then how about I list all the things you lied about last night."

I shake my head. "I don't know. There's really no reason to dredge up the past."

"Where do I start?" He ignores me and his eyes drop to my chest. His hand pulls through my hair, feeling its way down my side, landing low on my hip. "First, you lied about how much you loved my ass."

"I did not," I gasp. Of course, that's not a lie. He has a great ass. Addy told me he plays lacrosse in his spare time, so maybe that's it. It's muscular and, when he bends over behind the bar to reach for a bottle of wine, it's downright perfection.

I let out a whimper as his index finger circles my

nipple before making its way up to my collar bone. Hot on my skin, his touch drags back down between my breasts, parting the material where it barely hangs on.

"You did." He looks back up to my face. "That's a weird thing to lie about, little dandelion."

"Please, don't call me that," I whisper.

"Why?" His voice dips to match mine and I think he's going to lean in to kiss me, but he doesn't. I yelp when his hands come to my hips and he plops me up on the counter next to my double cheeseburger that's getting cold. "Did you lie about that, too? About the power of the sun, youthful joy, and ... what was the last one?"

My breath catches because I've totally screwed myself and I'm ninety-nine percent sure I spilled all my secrets last night. Secrets I haven't told my best friends—not even Addy.

"Oh yeah." He spreads my legs and steps between them, running his hands up the sides of my bare thighs. "Long-lasting happiness." His hands continue upward, pulling my kimono with them, and my eyes close at his touch.

"All lies," I breathe and my eyes fly open when he reaches the sides of my bare ass. The only thing between us is the light Asian silk I bought the last time I went to Chinatown. Its watercolor-hued threads are woven into a floral print with birds and a peacock.

He squeezes my ass cheeks and doesn't take his eyes off mine. "You're a naughty little liar."

Pulling my ass to the edge of the counter, he leans in to kiss me at the same time. I grip his shoulders to hang on and can't stop myself from wrapping my legs around the backs of his thighs as I teeter on the ledge. But I shouldn't worry, he holds me tight as he devours my mouth.

"You're bare under this." Unlike me—lying about not lying—he murmurs the truth against my lips before asking, "Do you have a headache?"

With his hands on my ass, I have no words. My head might be spinning from what he's doing to me, but the only thing that aches right now is below my waist, pressed against his erect cock.

I forget about everything—about all the time I've spent avoiding him and my father who abandoned me when I was little but now seems to be hell-bent on finding me—and throw caution to the tequila. I shake my head.

"You're really not going to answer any of my questions?"

I can't help but like the way he feels and my body hums. My words are clipped and thoughtless, just like the current state of my brain. "I told you—boring. Nothing to tell."

He pulls his head back and looks at me. His eyes roam my face first, then down to my body that he's completely taken over with his touch.

"I can't just leave you here like this, can I?" he asks.

Spinning in a whole new way that has nothing to do with the tequila, I look up and my only answer is my heels digging into the backs of his thighs and my fingernails into his shoulders. If he leaves me like this, I'll be forced to let the cheeseburger go cold and head straight for my vibrator.

I swear, his whiskey eyes darken before he leans in and his lips return to mine, a hypnotic pull so strong, it makes it hard to deny him.

I feel the pull of the silk tie that's precariously holding on as if its life depends on it, causing my kimono to fall open.

"Fuck." He looks down between us, his eyes dragging heavily over me. "You're more beautiful than I imagined."

He cups my breast again, this time skin-to-skin. Running his hand down the center of my body, never letting go of my ass with his other. When his index finger runs so lightly through my sex, it's the sweetest pain I've ever experienced.

I need more—so much more.

Never did I think I'd be here with Evan Charles Hargrove III. It doesn't matter how much I've secretly dreamed about it.

"So wet."

When I open my eyes, he looks from his hand to me as he slides a finger inside while his thumb brushes my clit.

"You were fighting this, Mary. Been fighting me off for so long—but no more. As of this moment," he presses on my clit, making me moan, as if he needed to do more to get my attention, "this is happening."

I ignore all the reasons that dance through my head as to why I've done everything in my power to ward off Evan's advances. I forget about the scum of the earth man who's back in Massachusetts looking for me. Instead, for once, I listen to my heart. To the one, selfish reason that should never cancel out all sense of reason— I want him. I want him now more than I've ever wanted anything.

I spread my legs farther.

As he watches, his tongue wets his lips in that way that secretly drives me wild. "There you go."

He plunges two fingers inside me—then three and, it feels so good, my head falls back. I have to let go of Evan to support myself on the counter. Arching into his touch, I chase my orgasm like a wild woman. He circles my clit with firm, slow strokes, bringing me close but not giving me nearly enough.

When I try to move against his hand, desperate for more, he lightens his touch. "You're fucking perfect. All this, just for me. Tell me that you get it."

I open my eyes and tip my head to look at him. Sitting here, bare and spread before him as he stands there fully dressed finger fucking me, I nod and my answer comes anxious and needy. "Yes. All yours."

"Finally," he utters before kissing me hard and turning his attention back to my clit.

This time, he's all business, working me into such a state, I only faintly hear myself call out when I come. My ears ring and my toes tingle as my body convulses against his hand. I feel his thick arm round my back to support my weight as he wrings me dry, leaving me in a limp pile of mush held tight to his body.

I sit in his arms, recovering, as the world comes back to me, my current state of nakedness hitting me as my senses sharpen. He strokes my hair, my back, my ass.

At the most inopportune time, my stomach audibly complains and I feel Evan smile against the side of my head.

Needing to change the subject to absolutely anything besides my past and the life-altering orgasm he just gave me, I ask, "Is that a Diet Coke?"

"Been watching you for what feels like forever. What else would I bring you?" He fists my hair, pulling my head just enough for me to see nothing but his golden-brown eyes. "No more tequila for you in the near future. And Mary?"

"Hmm?"

"I'm picking you up tonight. Be ready to talk."

I shake my head. "Tonight's poker night."

He pulls me in tight. "We'll skip."

If I go to poker, I don't have to talk to Evan. "No. I can't let Addy down. If we skip, it'll mess up the table."

He sighs. "Fine. I'll pick you up. We'll talk after poker."

I'll leave early for Addy's so I'll have my own car, make an excuse to leave, and head straight for Mexico.

I smile. "Sounds good to me."

5

KEEP MY MOUTH SHUT AND MY CLOTHES ON

Mary

I'M NOT QUITE sure how poker night came to be, but after I bonded with Addy the first time she sat in my chair at the salon, she insisted I attend. It's become an odd cluster of her employees and me.

Actually, they're all pretty normal and I'm the odd one, but I've always been on the outside looking in. It's not fun but after spending thirteen years bouncing around the foster care system, I know exactly what I am—a charity case. Never a family member, yet included out of sheer obligation. I am friends with Piper and her dad is sweet. He did everything he could to bring me into their little fold. But, by the time this happened, I was so used to being on the outside, it was hard to allow myself to be included. It was the "it's not you, it's me" thing.

Everything is my father's fault. Every-*freaking*-thing.

I hate being a charity case and I certainly don't need Evan nosing around in my business.

Evan has proven to be hypnotic. I knew if I gave in,

this would happen. I curse the moment I was weak and agreed to dinner. I was ignoring him like a champ—like the C-list rock star that I am. He teases me and I bite back with my words. He shoots me his sexy, private smirks and I roll my eyes. His private touches to my arm, hip, or the small of my back always earn him an elbow to the ribs.

He treats me like the secret he visualizes naked and I treat him like the enemy.

But he doesn't have to visualize me naked anymore after he swooned my robe right off of me this afternoon.

The last thing I need is to be held hostage by Evan at poker night.

But Evan proved how sly he is by reading my mind. I'm on my way out the door forty-five minutes early to avoid him but here he is, sauntering up the stairs to my second level apartment.

"You trying to skip out on me?"

I have no excuse so, for the first time since I was drunk last night, I tell the truth. "Yes. Yes, I am."

He has no response besides taking the two steps separating us and reaching around, placing his hand on my ass at the same moment his lips hit mine, reminding me he had me very much naked on my kitchen counter just a few short hours ago.

He's standing on the step below me and we're eye to eye. "We could skip poker. I'll order dinner and you can talk with your mouth full."

I shake my head. "No. Addy is expecting me—us. You know how Morris feels about not having enough players at the table."

"Okay. I'll wrap up the game early, but after that you need to be prepared to talk." I tense when my phone vibrates where it's tucked in my back pocket. And since that's where his hand is resting, Evan feels it, too. "Do you need to see who that is?"

I take a step back, which means taking a step up, and almost trip. He reaches out to steady me as I silence my phone. "Nope. I can check it later."

He stuffs one hand into his pocket and extends the other to me. "Then let's get this done so we can get out of there."

I don't take his hand. I sidestep him and speed down the stairs like the maniac I've turned into over the last twenty-four hours.

I DON'T DRINK anything at poker. Addy's new hot-guy neighbor, Crew, shows up and looks like he wants to devour her. Everyone could see it, so Evan doesn't have to work hard at wrapping up the game early.

Everyone bows out early and when we get back to my apartment, I don't even have to fake how tired I am. My hangover has wiped me out along with worry about why Piper has called me three times in the last two hours but, because a certain man has butted his way into my life, I haven't been able to take any of her calls.

I look over at Evan, who makes my small living room seem even smaller, and realize there's no way he's leaving anytime soon. I drop my purse on the sofa. "I'm going to change. Help yourself to what little is in the fridge."

He lifts his chin and takes the three steps to my kitchen. I hear him pop open a can of something as I shut myself in my room. I fall back on my bed, close my eyes, and wonder why my life can never be simple. I'm always clawing to keep up and, now with my dad looking for me and Evan pursuing me, my brain is on a never-ending merry-go-round. All I want to do is jump off and take a break from the dizzying ride.

Maybe I'll just lie here for a minute. If Evan wants to talk to me so badly, he can wait.

I grab my pillow. Just five minutes to rest my head will surely give me the willpower to deal with him.

And by deal, I mean keep my mouth shut and my clothes on.

6

ACCIDENTAL ALLIES

Evan

"WHAT'S TAKING SO long? You cleaning out your closet in there?"

I'm standing in front of a wobbly bookcase filled with books and ridiculousness. It's wallpapered with inappropriate bumper stickers, cut-out memes, and raunchy cartoons. She's got the entire cast of the Harry Potter bobble head collection. I'm pretty sure there's about a hundred other figurines and, as I inspect her rag-tag collection of paperbacks, it looks like Mary has a penchant for smut. Every cover is well used and shows more skin than fabric.

I take another drink of my Diet Coke, which is about all she has in her refrigerator, and turn for her bedroom. "Mary. It's really gonna hurt my feelings if you snuck out the window."

I knock on her door and get nothing, then put my hand on the doorknob and turn it. It's not like I didn't see everything this afternoon when she practically wrote me a formal invitation to make her body sing.

How ironic is it that I got her naked in her kitchen but every time I see the woman in bed, she's fully clothed and dead to the world. At least tonight she isn't drunk and I shouldn't be surprised she's out like a light. She yawned all through poker and her eyes still looked like she was on the tequila struggle bus. Her hair, that I can't stop fixating on, is pulled out of its tie. In a mess of colorful waves, it floats behind her in freezeframe. She's perfect.

I lean onto the doorjamb and take in her tiny frame curled into a pillow where she lies sideways across her small double bed. Her room is even more eccentric than her bookcases. She's got beads hanging in front of her windows, a million pillows are stacked in the corner, and her floor is covered in clothes and shoes.

Mary is messy. And I love it.

She's filled her world with as much color as she puts in her hair and I have to fight my cock from swelling from just being here. I want to learn everything there is to know about her.

I want to wake her up, have her talk to me, force her to trust me, and then make her come again, but with my tongue this time. I want to do all kinds of things but I know I need to prove myself to her first.

Her purse rings from the other room and I pull her door shut so it doesn't wake her. Digging through her bag —which is as messy as her bedroom—I unearth her phone through loose mints, tampons, and crinkled receipts.

There's a picture of Mary with a blonde on the screen. They've got their arms around each other with their lips puckered into a kiss for the selfie. Weird. All the screen says is *Piper*.

I slide my finger across the screen. "Hello?"

I get nothing before a female voice snaps at me. "Who is this?"

"Evan. Who is this?"

She doesn't give me her name. "This is Mary's number and has been for years. Where is she?"

Whoever this is, she's protective of Mary. I can tell she'd jump through this phone and strangle me if she could.

I sit down on the old sofa covered in throw blankets and stretch my legs out, propping them on top of the chipped coffee table. "Mary's asleep. Who's this?"

"But, it's not even ten o'clock there. Mary's a night owl. Why is she asleep, why are you there while she's asleep, and why are you answering her phone?"

I lean my head back on the sofa. "That's a lot of whys."

"I'm not shitting you. I know Mary's at home because I just tracked her on Snapchat. If you don't tell me who you are right now and why you're there, I'm gonna call the police. Or you can just wake her up and put her on the phone so I know she's okay." She takes a breath and rethinks her demands. "In fact, do that. Wake her up and put her on the phone."

She sounds about as threatening as a kitten. "I'm not waking her. She's tired. Are you the one who's been lighting up her phone last night and tonight? She won't answer it around me."

"Wait." The woman pauses and her voice turns just slightly less frantic. "You're the date from last night?"

"Depends. If she had good things to say, then, yes. If not, I have no clue who she went out with last night."

Her tone turns nosy. "Your name is Evan?"

"Yeah and just to finish off the Spanish Inquisition, my last name is Hargrove, I work for Mary's friend Addy at the winery, and just to calm your ass down, I've never been arrested. Taken into custody? Sure, once in high school when I was stopped with two kegs in the back of my car. But I got out of it."

That earns her a small laugh. "What, is your dad a police officer?"

"Nope. But he does sit on the city council so he can make sure no one builds a big-box store next to our property."

"Interesting."

"Trust me, it's not. Who are you?"

"I'm Mary's best friend, Piper. It was nice chatting with you but I need to talk to Mary and I needed to do it hours ago."

"I want to talk to her, too, but she needs the sleep. I'm not waking her."

She sighs. "I don't know why, but there's something about you ... even all the way from Massachusetts, my gut tells me to trust you."

"Your gut would be right. Maybe you and I should cut out the middleman and have a chat while my sleeping mermaid catches up on her beauty rest."

She says nothing, but I hear her shifting the phone. Finally, she asks, "You're a friend of Addy's?"

"Yeah. A friend and an employee. It's how I met Mary."

Piper seems to be contemplating just how trustworthy I might be. "Mary loves Addy. I'm almost jealous because, even though Mary moved away years ago, I miss her."

I cock my head and start putting things together. "You're from Massachusetts?"

"Yes. From Boston. Mary and I were inseparable."

"Last night Mary opened up about something from her past and I can tell she's worried. You know anything about that?"

"Evan," she calls for me even though I'm right here and she knows it. "You're there and are able to watch out for her. I'm here and have all the information. I think we might need each other."

I look to the closed bedroom door and wonder what the hell is going on with the sleeping woman behind it. I think I might've just found my in with Mary.

"Accidental allies," I state. "Tell me what I need to know. I'm willing to do whatever's necessary to pave the road for her and me."

Her tone turns sing-songy. "That's so sweet. I can't wait to tell her that."

I think about this afternoon when I had her bared to me. "Trust me. She knows. Now, tell me everything."

And Mary's friend with the strange name proceeds to blow my mind.

7

BARREL-OF-MONKEYS KIND
OF FUN

Mary

I WAKE UP in my own bed without a hangover.

Look at me, winning at life.

I am, however, still in the same clothes I wore last night. And next to me is my cell phone and a hand-written note folded into a tent on my pillow with my name scribbled across the front.

After I rub my eyes, I unfold it.

It's six in the morning. Yeah, I stayed all night. I didn't want to wake you and, for the second night in a row, I enjoyed watching you sleep. Call me creepy, I don't give a shit. I learned a lot while you were snoozing away last night. I also drank all your Diet Coke and checked your schedule book. I know you work today, so I'll be back tonight at seven. I'm bringing you a case of Diet Coke so you don't fall asleep on me again. We're going to talk about Massachusetts, your fucking jackass of a father, and then you're going to pack a bag because you're not

staying in your apartment any longer until we know where he
is. You only have a double bed. I have a queen. I win.
By the way, you're just as beautiful when you sleep as you are
when you're glaring at me and as you are when you're naked
and moaning for me.
Don't make me wait.
Evan

One thing is certain—the man is verbose.

Another thing that is even more certain—I will *not* be in my apartment at seven o'clock.

And damn him for drinking all my Diet Coke!

———

TWELVE HOURS HAVE PASSED. The clock is hanging over my head like a ticking time bomb. I know Evan works in the tasting room until six every day and sometimes stays later.

I called Piper while my client's highlights were processing and she spilled the beans about how she spilled *all the beans* to Evan while I slept. She told me the whole thing and showed no remorse because, in her words, "Your fucking father found out where you live. Someone at the bar told Jake right away and informed him that Duane Giesen jumped into a creaky old Chevy with rusted out bumpers and headed east."

I told her I couldn't believe my childhood friend betrayed me by spilling all my dirty laundry to a stranger, to which she replied, "I love Evan! I can't wait to meet him. He made me promise that Jake and I would visit soon and he said he'd take care of our accommodations. I'm so mad that you didn't tell me how amazing he is. I feel so much better after talking to him last night. I know he's going to do everything he can to watch out for you."

See? Total betrayal.

Then I got a call from Addy and, after she made an appointment for a Keratin treatment, she basically chewed my ass for holding out on her about my father looking for me. Of course, blabbermouth Evan told her everything. She's so sweet, she actually made *me* feel bad that I hadn't told her sooner. Before we hung up, I had apologized and promised that if I didn't feel safe, I'd come and stay in her guestroom since she has about two million of them in her big-ass farmhouse.

Great. On top of having to avoid Evan, and how I feel bad about Addy, I'm annoyed that Piper is so happy for me. But I can't help but wonder what accommodations Evan was talking about.

I'm exhausted.

I look up at the clock and wish I could turn into a pumpkin when I see it click over to seven. I've stayed at the salon longer than necessary—I've swept and cleaned every station, washed and dried all the towels, and cleaned out my drawers. I hate staying late but, after my day, I'll do anything to avoid Evan.

My phone dings from across the room. I walk to my station, plop into my chair, and brace. When I open my messages, I'm right. It's him.

Evan – Why are you avoiding me?

Me – I'm not. I'm at Addy's. We're making jelly.

Wow. I'm really going to go to hell for lying so much.

Evan – No you're not. I just called Addy and she didn't know where you were.

Me – She's too preoccupied with Crew. He's totally into

*her. I'm with Bev and we're in Addy's kitchen cleaning
rhubarb. You know we come and go as we want.*

Evan – Bullshit.

*Me – Look, I'm good for the night. I don't know what my
so-called best friend said to you, but she's dramatic. Whatever
it was, it's not a big deal and I'm pretty sure she lied to you.*

*Evan – It is a big deal. It's a huge deal and I looked into
your dad after what Piper told me last night. None of it's
good. It's all really bad.*

I need to quit texting so I'll quit lying.

*Me – I gotta go. We're out of sugar and I need to run to
the store.*

Evan – Bullshit.

Me – No, it's true. All out of sugar.

Evan – Turn around.

What?

I put my toe to the floor and twirl my chair to find him
standing at the door. He's sliding his damn cell into his
pocket and hits the glass with his flat, open palm. "Open
the door."

I'm never going to get away from him.

I get up, trudge across the room, and grab the keys off
the desk. When I flip the lock and open the door, he
doesn't move. "You know, you're a real killer to a guy's
confidence."

I shake my head and close my eyes. I'm done playing.
And lying. When I open my eyes, I'm as serious as I've
ever been when I beg, "Please, Evan. I can't do this with
you. Not right now. Whatever Piper told you today is true
but she didn't tell you everything because she doesn't
know everything. You don't want to be with me. I know I
look like I'm a barrel-of-monkeys kind of fun, but you'll

come to your senses eventually and I'm not sure if I can take that slap of reality. Not with you. I need you to stay my frenemy. Addy and all of you at the vineyard, you're all I have here. If it gets weird between you and me, I'll be the one to go because I'm already on the outside. I always have been and I always will be."

He holds the door that's still standing open and, between his gaze and the evening air, I shiver.

He lowers his voice and I'm not sure I've ever heard him so serious. "I'd never do that. Not to you, Mary."

I shake my head. "No, you wouldn't do that on purpose because you're the perfect, all-American guy with all the fireworks, but it could still happen. It is the way it is and we wouldn't be able to stop it."

He holds out his hand. "Give me one night to change your mind. One night is all I need. Come with me."

I nibble on my bottom lip because he makes it seem so easy when everything is excruciatingly difficult. It always has been.

"You have to give me a chance to prove it to you. I know you will because it's who you are. It's why I want you."

I sigh.

"Open yourself up to me. I swear, you won't regret it." He means it because he's good to the bone. I've watched him and, even after all the teasing and heckling to get my attention, I know it to be true.

"Let me get my purse and lock up."

His face transforms. Not in arrogance because he's gotten what he wanted. No.

Evan Hargrove is relieved.

I don't know what he has planned but the man is

smoother than a freshly-waxed upper lip. I certainly need to be on guard and definitely—most *definitely*—keep my clothes on.

8

MATCH MADE IN HELL

Evan

"ARE WE NOT going back to your apartment?"

Keeping my eyes on the dark country road, I shake my head. "I've decided if I want the upper hand, I need to keep you on your toes and alert so we're going on a field trip. I don't need you sneaking off to take a nap."

She's not getting away from me again. Now that I know what her problem is, I don't want her at her apartment anyway. She didn't pack a bag like I told her to, but that's okay. I'll have anything she could need where I'm taking her.

All I know is I'm done fucking around with this cat-and-mouse shit. That's over. Especially after our time in her kitchen yesterday. No way is she running away from me again.

"I need to be home early. I have appointments first thing in the morning."

"Nice try. I'm on to you." I glance over at her before I

turn and pull up to the gate, rolling down my window. "I memorized your schedule. You don't go in 'til tomorrow afternoon."

She shakes her head. "I have another headache."

I can't help but smile. She's ridiculous. "How about I promise to make you ache in other places?"

Her gaze jerks to me, her vibrant long hair flips across the back of her seat as she widens her eyes. I don't know whether to laugh or kiss her.

"Where are we?" she asks.

I key in the code and wait for the gates to part. "My parents' house."

"Evan, please. I don't want to be here."

I pull through the heavily-secured entrance onto the property. "We're not going to their house. I'm taking you to the barns. I still don't know everything about your dad, but if it's as bad as you make it out to be, he won't find you here, not that he could step foot on this land, it's so secure."

She doesn't say a word but sits beside me looking so worried, you'd think I was driving her to the guillotine.

"Relax, Mary. My parents aren't home, not that we'd see them if you didn't want to." What I don't tell her is they're in the South of France for the next month. I park and move to get out. "I promise there won't be any other humans in sight."

When I go around to open her door, she's sitting there with her arms crossed and her leg bouncing with nervous energy. She's biting her lip in a way that makes me jealous. I hold my hand out. "Come. It'll be just you and me. I want to show you something."

She closes her eyes and sighs. "Okay, but you have to take me home tonight."

I don't agree to that, shut her door, and take a second to enjoy the view as she walks ahead of me toward one of the barns. She's downright tiny and her hair is so long, it swishes as she walks even pulled back. Her fine ass, that I'm now well acquainted with, fits in my hands like it was made for me, and makes me hungrier for her now more than ever.

I grab her hand. "Had you not turned instantly wet for me yesterday, I might think you don't like me."

"Can we not talk about that?" She doesn't try to pull her hand from mine and a blush creeps up her fair skin. "Wow. I had no idea barns could be so fancy."

This farm has been in my family for three generations. Hargrove Farms is one of the largest thoroughbred breeders on the east coast. I lived here my whole life until I moved out for college, so I rarely think about the opulence I grew up around. Sliding the door open, I lead her through the bay with stalls on either side. "All barns probably smell the same, so I apologize for that."

We walk through the long aisle to my target. I let go of her long enough to slide open the door to the stall and we hear him before we see him—our newest foal born just last month.

I go to his mom first and look back to Mary. "Come meet Narnia. She's mine and so gentle, she was made to be a mom. She comes from impeccable blood lines. This is her ninth foal."

Mary approaches slowly. Since I doubt she's been around horses before, I take her hand and lift it to Narnia's forehead.

"See?" I move behind Mary and wrap my arm around her. "Let her smell you and then she'll trust you around her baby."

Mary strokes Narnia and, despite her actions earlier, leans into me and sighs. "I knew you came from a lot, but not all this."

I put my lips to her ear. "We're not that different, you know."

Mary huffs and shakes her head. "Said the guy who grew up on an estate and is the son of a horse breeder."

The colt appears, dipping his head under his mother's neck and nudges at us with his nose, giving us a nicker. Mary laughs for the first time since she was drunk and loose the other night. "He's so cute. What's his name?"

"He'll be given a formal name for the jockey club when he turns one. I'm sure he'll earn a nickname as his personality develops."

The foal crowds Mary, nuzzling her, and I step back to watch. Standing there in her flip-flops and cut-off jean shorts, topped with a vintage Nirvana T-shirt, she might seem out of place. After last night, I know for a fact she's worried about our worlds colliding. But I've never seen anyone I want more.

I lean against the stall and stuff my hands in my pockets. "When I was five, my mom OD'ed on painkillers."

She turns her head, giving me her big blue eyes. "What?"

I shrug. "I was the one who found her. She was lying naked on her bathroom floor. Luckily, the maid was there. I guess she'd been strung out for years but I was too young to know the difference. I figured everyone's mom slept their days away. She spent years in and out of rehab. I got old enough to realize that wasn't normal."

Mary's face softens. "I'm so sorry." She turns back to the foal who's demanding her attention. "Why did you tell me that?"

"You think we're different. You think we don't belong together. And, by the way, in your drunken state, you told me I wasn't weird enough for you."

The foal grows bored, moves away, and Mary turns to face me. "Well, that wasn't a lie. You're like," she throws her hand out to me, "barely weird at all. Whereas my weirdness is off the charts."

I push away from the wall and take her hand to pull her out of the stall. "You're not weird. You're colorful."

"Too colorful for you and your horses and your estate."

I secure the barn door and push her up against the wall. When I tip her head to me, her face is masked with everything I hate. Uncertainty. Dread. Fear. "I know about your past. Piper told me everything. Your dad's an asshole and your mom died a meth head."

She grabs onto my shirt, but not to push me away. She hangs on tight as her eyes well. "I hate that you know that about me. I did everything I could to get away from that life and everyone who knew me then. I don't tell anyone about that part of me."

"You are not them. You're no more your mom than I am mine. My mom finally got better and beat it, but it doesn't erase the past. We're not our parents, Mary. We have no boundaries. No definitions of who we have to be. Not unless you lay those on us and, if you do, I'll be pissed."

Her clear blue eyes gaze up at me and I can tell she's trying to make a decision, though, in the end, I know there's no choice. Not when she reacts the way she does. She wants this as much as I do, she just needs to quit fighting herself.

I slide my hand under the hem of her T-shirt and tease her smooth skin, watching her face change by the second.

She settles into my touch and her eyes fall as she shakes her head. "I don't know. I have a feeling this isn't a good idea."

I let my hand settle on her skin and grip her hip to get her attention. "Why do you think your dad is looking for you now? Piper explained that he's bad news and told me about all the trouble he's been in."

"I have no idea. He's made a career of getting women hooked on anything they'd try. When they become desperate, he pimps them out and they're happy to do it for their next fix. That's what happened to my mom even though I barely remember her. Everyone who knew my mom was only too happy to inform me where I came from. Our worlds, Evan ... they couldn't be more different."

I move to kiss her and murmur against her lips, "That might be his world but it's not yours."

She doesn't turn away from my kiss. "It's not that simple."

"It is." I slide my hand up her back and pop the hook on her bra. "Don't carry the weight of your father's sins. I want you to stay here with me tonight. Just you and me. Tell me you don't want it."

Her eyes go wide. "Evan."

"Guess I need to convince you." I pull her bra away from her body and, just like in her kitchen, I cup her tit and give it a squeeze. Lust-driven, her lids fall heavy over her blue eyes and my dick swells.

"Convince me of what?" she breathes.

"That the idea of us could be the best thing that's ever happened."

I kiss her and allow my tongue to invade her mouth. I've wanted her for so long. I took advantage of a talkative Mary the other night when she drank too much. I made her fess up about why she thinks we shouldn't be together. It was then she told me bits of what her fucking parents put her through and Piper pieced the rest together. It's nothing short of a miracle she survived that unscathed, let alone turned out as perfect as she is today.

I let her mouth go and my fingers work the button on her shorts. "The other night you rambled on about dandelions."

She shakes her head and stops my hands. "Please forget about the dandelions—and we can't do this here. Aren't there people around? Don't your parents have a ... I don't know, butler or something?"

I shake my head. "Told you my parents weren't home and they don't have a butler. It's late so the trainers and handlers are gone for the day. It's you, me, and twenty-nine horses. There're some barn cats around, too, but they don't like people. I'm sure the animals won't care when I go down on you."

Her eyes go big. "You can't do that to me here in the barn."

I put my lips to her as I finally get her shorts undone. "I can. After yesterday in your kitchen, I can't wait another second. I have to taste you."

Not messing around, I push her panties down with her shorts and cup her between the legs. She's wet again. So fucking wet it makes my mouth water and I have to adjust my cock.

Mary's head falls back with a small thud.

"Oh." She moans when I drag a finger between her

legs and drop to my knees where I'm at eye level with her clit.

I look up and keep teasing her with the tip of my index finger. "Did you know that the clitoris is the only human organ whose sole purpose is to provide sexual gratification?"

She frowns and tries to rub her thighs together. "Are you seriously talking to me about my clit?"

I nod, leaning in to kiss her bare hip. "I promise to always be serious about your clit. After the other day, I think I might be obsessed with it."

"Please stop talking," she begs even though she shifts her hips forward for more of my touch.

"Love that you're smooth for me, Mary. You've got the prettiest pussy. I could look at it for the rest of my life."

"I, um..." she stutters. "Don't like body hair. I'm sort of fanatical about waxing."

"Lucky me." I untangle her clothes from her feet and throw one of her legs over my shoulder. Looking up at her, I lick my lips. "Baby, I plan on breaking down all your walls, so lean back and enjoy it."

Then, I do what I wanted to do in her kitchen and again last night before she fell asleep—hell, what I've wanted since the moment I laid eyes on her. Her T-shirt has nothing on the nirvana lying between her legs. I lick up from her center to her clit and she grabs onto my hair and gasps. When I suck her into my mouth she thrusts her hips forward, offering me everything and I take it. With one hand on her ass to hold her still, I lift her leg higher and devour her.

So fucking sweet. I've come to love my wine, but Mary on my tongue is something far more potent.

But this? Her?

I feel it. She holds me, lock and key. I'm her prisoner.

Mary is my vice.

Between fucking her with my tongue and consuming every inch of her pussy, she starts to rock against my mouth. Her whimpers, shallow breaths, and moans of my name echo off the limestone walls of the barn. It's the sweetest symphony I've ever heard.

When she comes I have to support her weight as her body convulses and she spasms on my mouth. That goes straight to my dick and if I don't have her soon, I'll explode.

Without letting her go, I stand, yank her T-shirt up and off, along with her bra. "You're so fucking perfect."

In her post orgasmic bliss, she lifts her sexy eyes to mine. "I've dreamed of you but never thought it could happen."

I pick her up and it takes her a tick for her to lift her languid arms and legs around me. With one hand at her ass, I pull the tie on her hair, letting her colorful locks fall around us. "I might eat you out in the barn, but I'm not fucking you here for the first time. We're going to the guest house."

She rubs her pussy against my aching cock but her words are nothing but pure sarcasm. "Of course. I should've assumed you'd have guest quarters. I was crazy to think we don't fit—what with me growing up in a crack house, my dad whoring out my mom, and me being bumped around in foster care. We're a match made in hell, Evan."

I frown and pull her head back so I can look into her eyes. "I'm gonna fuck those thoughts right out of your head. Don't ever utter them again."

I turn the corner and she shivers in my arms from the

cool night air as I make the short walk through the darkness to the building next door that my parents converted into guest quarters for breeders and buyers.

I punch in the master code to the electronic lock and turn the knob. Flipping on the lights, I still in the entryway when my eyes catch us in the mirror. Mary is naked and wrapped around me, her fair skin a stark contrast to my tan arms from riding and lacrosse. But it's the skin above her ass that gets my attention.

"What's this?" Her body tightens as I run my fingers over the small of her back where the ends of her hair tease my fingers.

She frowns before turning to look over her shoulder. When her eyes meet mine in the mirror, she exhales in a huff—a loss for words.

I grip her ass. "This means something and you're telling me now so when I'm looking down at this while I'm fucking you, it'll mean something to me, too."

9

GAME OVER

Mary

TENSE IN his arms.

"I'm serious, Mary. If you inked this on your skin, it means something, not just some drunken ramblings. I want to know before I take you for the first time."

I look over my shoulder to our reflection. With the dark of night framing us from behind, only the light from the fancy sconces on either side of the mirror brightens our space. I'm naked, wrapped around Evan's muscular body where he's holding me easily, his hand squeezing my ass.

His eyes are on my lower back, specifically on the colorful art that decorates my skin. I got the tattoo the day I turned eighteen and was no longer a ward of the state. It looks painted on with bright watercolors in hues of greens, purples, teals, and golds. A dandelion with seeds blowing across my back. I saved up for it, planned it for years leading up to my freedom.

Freedom.

Between my fucked-up parents, the equally fucked-up foster care system, and me trying to survive, I never had a day of it until I turned eighteen.

His eyes catch mine in the mirror and I press my sex into his cock—the rough denim of his jeans biting into my sensitive skin and over stimulated clit from his charmed tongue and lips. All this time I fantasized about that tongue but I never did it justice. His mouth between my legs was pure paradise.

"It's a dandelion," I say.

He raises a brow. "No shit. Why do you love them so much?"

I turn away from the mirror and all I see are shadowed whiskey eyes. "When I was put in foster care for the first time, the woman was nice—the nicest I ever had. I was so little but I'll never forget what she said. She called me a pretty little dandelion who grew up out of the cracked pavement. Then she said most people think dandelions are weeds and crush their happy spirit, but she thought they were beautiful and only needed the warmth of the sun to grow. She was the best foster mom I ever had but the courts gave me back to my dad after just a couple weeks. I never saw her again but I'll never forget her. My tattoo means I'm free."

His arms constrict around me and I'm crushed to his chest. "Baby. Everything you mumbled to me in your drunken state makes sense. At least I had my dad. You had no one."

Suddenly it isn't just my state of nakedness that has me feeling bare. "I was enough—I had to be. I survived. I'm fine now."

He kicks the door shut behind us and starts to move.

The next thing I know, I'm lying on bedding so soft, it's a whispered kiss to my skin. Evan reaches behind him and pulls a condom out of his pocket and tosses it on the bed next to me.

"From now on, you're not gonna be *fine*. It'll be my mission to make sure you're way more than *fine*, Mary. And I'm gonna start by making you mine."

He's right. I've done my best to avoid him from the first day I met him at Whitetail Farms. Guys like him don't end up with girls like me. Sure, they might enjoy time with me because I'm fun or edgy, but they always end up with a woman who's comfortable maneuvering her way around the social webs of a country club or, in Evan's case, the Kentucky Derby.

"Waited all this time for you," he murmurs as he looks down at me after he rips his shirt off and makes quick work of his jeans. "You think we're a match made in hell— if that's the case, we'll light it on fire together because this is happening."

I take a breath and reach for him, pulling him to me so his mouth lands on mine. He needs to stop talking. I'm not sure how much more I can take.

As if proving it with his kiss, he consumes and possesses me. It's as if every additional touch from Evan means exponentially more than the last. I thought I was obsessed before, but I'm in deep now.

I reach for the condom and move to sit up, forcing him to stand in front of me. Reaching into his boxers, I free his cock. It's thick, veined, perfect, and glistens on the tip—all for me.

I want him.

Peeking up at him through the dim light, I fist him at the base and lean in, giving him a flick with my tongue.

His salty precum makes my mouth water. Gripping the condom I was about to roll on him, the foil crinkles in my hand as I pull him into my mouth.

"Fuck, baby." Evan pulls my hair gently, holding my head as he takes over, sliding his cock into my mouth. I peek up again when he pulls out to the tip and gives me his eyes. "If you're good with your mouth on top of everything else, I might just fall in love with you."

I gasp at his words but he doesn't give me a chance to catch my breath. He thrusts his hips forward and fills my mouth, the tip of his cock touching the back of my throat. He fucks my mouth as I suck, loving every inch of him.

He groans and grips my hair tighter, pulling out. Yanking the condom from my hand, he tears it with his teeth and sheaths himself. I start to lie back, wanting him more than anything, but he shakes his head. "No. After what you just told me, I want to look at the symbol that makes you *you*."

He flips me over on my hands and knees, spanning my hips and lower back with his big hands before reaching down to tease my clit. I push back—wanting more, needing him.

I toss my hair over my shoulder and look back. "Evan. Please."

His gaze moves from my tat to my face, those soulful brown eyes settling on me. He thrusts inside, stretching me with a delicious ache I could become addicted to.

"You're not on your own anymore, baby." He slides a hand where my skin is inked before gripping my hip. "You've got me now. I'm not going anywhere."

I close my eyes as he starts to take me hard. I do my best to push back to meet him, to give a little of what he's giving me, but he's controlling it. His fingers bite into my skin with a possession I can feel down to my toes.

"Come here." He stops to pull me up, my back to his front as he supports my weight with a strong arm wrapped around me. Still impaled on him, he takes my hand in his and directs it between my legs. With our fingers dancing together, he puts his lips to my ear. "Come on my cock, baby. I want to feel you inside and out."

It doesn't take long with him moving my fingers over my clit. It's almost too much, yet my body searches for it.

"Oh," I breathe and he circles my fingers faster.

When I start to convulse on his cock, he moves, holding me tight and thrusting up into me as my orgasm rocks my body.

"Fuck, yes, baby." His breath comes heavy against my hair as he groans with his release. With his arms tightening impossibly hard around me, he puts his lips to my ear and his next words will remain laced in my heart forever. "No more cat-and-mouse shit. Game over, Mary. You're mine."

I open my eyes and turn to peek into his, filled with the same promise as his words.

"Tell me you get it and you'll stop fighting this. I've waited too long," he goes on.

I exhale and feel him surrounding me, his body covering mine like a shield. I've never had a protector, not really. My parents never gave a shit about me and I was just an extra paycheck to every foster parent I was placed with.

"Mary." He presses into me as his voice grows more impatient.

I can't even muster the words because for some reason saying them out loud is too much to bear.

I nod and hate that my eyes well at the same moment.

I'm glad I don't try to blink them back. If I had, I would have missed the relief that washes over his rugged features.

And I'll never forget this moment for the rest of my life.

I just gave myself to Evan in every way and I want to remember it forever.

10

EXPECTATIONS

Evan

I HEAR THE shower as soon as I walk into the guest house. Mary doesn't drink coffee, but she's always got a Diet Coke in her hand. I went to the fridge in the barn that we keep stocked for the handlers and trainers and got her one.

I'll stop and get her some breakfast on our way to her apartment. I hate that she can't come to the winery to be with me. She has clients later today.

I hear her phone vibrate in her bag and dig through it. Frowning, I wonder who could be calling from New York.

I know taking her for the first time last night still doesn't give me permission to answer her phone. But after, while we were in bed and before we found sleep, she told me more about how she grew up. She talked a lot and opened up and it was all I could do not to get up, track down her motherfucking father, and wrap my hands around his neck. I've never felt the urge to hurt anyone before, not like that.

I wish I could erase it all from her head. Hell, I wish I could erase him completely from her past.

I learned a lot last night. Like the only reason she escaped rape as a twelve-year-old girl at one of her foster homes was because a neighbor heard her cries and did something about it. It might not have happened but, from her tone and the way she described what she went through, I can tell the experience still haunts her to this day. Her telling me things like that might not give me the right to invade her privacy, but I'm gonna do it anyway.

"Hello?" I answer.

There's a pause before a male voice hits me from across the line. "Is Mary Giesen available?"

I feel my brows pucker. I move out of the bedroom and shut the door so she can't hear me if she gets out of the shower and walk over to the back doors that are floor to ceiling glass, looking out over the rolling hills of my family's property. I do everything I can to keep my tone only mildly irritated. "She can't come to the phone right now. Who's this?"

From everything I've learned from Mary and now, my new number one informant Piper, this is not how I expected her father to be contacting her, let alone sound like. His voice turns inquisitive. "I've been trying to get hold of Ms. Giesen for a couple of weeks. I've been leaving messages at this number and at the last place of employment I have on record for her. She hasn't returned my calls."

"I'm sorry," I lie. I'm not the least bit sorry and I'm pretty sure my voice reflects that. "Who are you and what do you want with Mary?"

"My name is Joe Ratcliff. I'm an attorney with Wilson Partners in Lexington. My business is with Ms. Giesen and, by law, I cannot divulge anything about the client I represent to anyone but her."

I note his full name and practice so I can look into him later. I might even call in a favor to my father's attorney—see what he can come up with. "I'll have her call you."

"Please do. Time is of the essence. It will behoove Ms. Giesen to return my call as soon as possible."

I disconnect the call and head back into the bedroom. She's pulling the clean tee over her head that I gave her to wear home that I had stored in my gym bag.

Seeing my shirt hang on her small body where it hits her halfway down her bare thighs, I want nothing more than to ignore the world and throw her back into bed. She looks from my hands to me. "What are you doing with my phone and is that Diet for me?"

I smirk and pop the top of the can, taking a sip before handing it to her. "You need to learn to drink coffee."

Her face twists and she shakes her head at the same time she nabs her phone out of my hand. "No way. I can't stomach the taste."

"You had a call."

She unlocks her phone and then looks up to me. "It doesn't say I missed a call."

I shrug. "That's because I answered it."

Her eyes narrow and her hand goes to her hip. "Don't you have a phone of your own? You sure seem to like to talk on mine."

"Why is an attorney from Lexington looking for you? He said he's left you messages. What else is going on?"

She shakes her head and turns to toss her phone in her bag. "He called again? I have no idea what that guy wants. Look at me, Evan." She holds her arms out low before she starts to pull on her shorts from yesterday. "Do

I look like someone who gets calls from attorneys? It can't be good so I haven't returned his calls."

I lean onto the door jamb and cross my arms. "So you're ignoring him? He's not the Feds, baby. Not much an attorney can do to you. It sounded important—you should call him."

She buttons her cut-off jean shorts and walks over to me. "You seemed into me yesterday, but before you hang your hat too long on my hook, you should know that I don't *adult*. At all. You saw my apartment. I had most of that crap when I was still in high school and I have no plans of replacing any of it with anything even close to grown up—let alone coordinating. I do hair, nails, and makeup for a living because it's basically like playing dress up. Sorry, but if you're into me, this is what you're gonna get."

I push off the wall, go to her, and park it on the edge of the bed. Tagging her hand, I pull her to stand between my legs. "You dropped everything to stay with Addy a few months ago when she was sick. You took Bev to a doctor's appointment. Hell, you even babysat Clara's kids and we all know what a sacrifice that is."

We're face-to-face and she reaches up to toy with my hair while nibbling at her lip. "That has nothing to do with my *Harry Potter* bobble head collection and my lack of adultness."

"Hey, look at me," I call for her. When her eyes hit mine, they're guarded. I thought we got past all this last night. "Do you know why I want you?"

Her chest rises against mine where I'm holding her tight. "For the life of me, no. We couldn't be more different."

"Because of the way you give to everyone around you.

You don't see it but they do and that's why they're drawn to you. That's why I can't get enough of you. I'm going to bust my ass to give you just a little bit of what you do for everyone else and start by looking into that attorney. If I find out he's on the up-and-up and has nothing to do with your father, you need to find out what he wants."

She ignores all the stuff about the attorney. "You can't get enough of me?"

"You've done a bang-up job ignoring me. Finally had to make a move 'cause I was tired of you always giving me the cold shoulder."

Her eyes well again and it hits me in a spot I've never experienced before. A place I didn't even know I had.

"This is happening?" she whispers.

It's not just a question, but a doubt—a disbelief.

I lean in to put my lips on hers. "Last night was not for nothing. If I have to tell you every day, I will. Yes."

She literally climbs my body and the next thing I know, her small frame is wrapped around me. I couldn't pry her off if I wanted to, which I don't. At this point, I think I'd be content if we could stay here forever.

But we can't live in the guest house.

I mean, we could but then my mother would be all up in our business. She's going to be obsessed with Mary as it is. As much as my dad was always on my ass to work for the family business, my mother only wants me to settle down. She's bored and enjoys a distraction. It's harmless now, but it comes from her addictive personality. I need to prepare Mary for that.

But not today.

One step at a time. I don't need my mother scaring Mary away with talk of weddings and grandbabies. I need to do everything I can to hook Mary deep before my mother has a chance to frighten her off, especially when she finds out Mary's never had a mom—not a real one anyway. Hell, I didn't either until I was seven but mine has made up for it since then.

"I have to go to work," Mary mumbles into my neck where her face is pressed. "But I don't want to. I want to stay here with you and your horses and pretend my dad isn't on his way to Virginia for who knows what and that I don't have strange lawyers trying to get hold of me."

I give her a squeeze. "I'm going to call my dad's attorney. He's a family friend so he should at least look into it for me. If that guy's legit, you can call him back. Then we'll figure out what your father wants and kick him the hell out of town. If he lives up to his reputation and stresses you out like this, he's not sticking around if I can help it. When was the last time you saw him?"

She leans back and sighs. "I ran into him in Boston right after I graduated from high school. At a gas station of all places. He barely recognized me at first but I didn't escape that easily. He kept trying to contact me after that —I was eighteen, not a ward of the state any longer, and he'd just gotten out of prison. I was already thinking about leaving Massachusetts and that was the last straw. I moved here and you know the rest."

I look at the clock on the bedside table. "I need to get you home so we can get to work. I'll try to get off early but you'll be around people all day. You'll be fine. I'll let you know what I find out from my dad's attorney and we'll go from there. Check one thing off the list."

She leans into me and puts her lips on my jaw and I regret the fact I can't lie back and let her lips do other things to me so I can return the favor. She finally relents. "Fine."

I tuck my hand up her shirt and splay my fingers across her tattoo I've become fixated on. "It's going to be more than *fine*. I promise."

When she gives me her eyes again, they're resigned and she lifts her slim shoulder. "There's no need to make me promises, Evan. My expectations in life are low. I'll deal with whatever happens, I just don't want you getting caught up in the drama that is my life."

I stand up with her in my arms and flip her to her back on the bed. Leaning over her, I crush my lips to hers, taking her mouth in a surprising yet bruising kiss. She hangs onto my neck and I let her up for air. "It's time to up your expectations, baby. And I swear to you, I'll meet every last one of them."

11

EGO

Mary

"MARY, DO YOU have time for a walk-in?"

I pull the curling wand from the last section of my client's hair and reach for my volume boosting spray. I shake my head and speak without looking away from my art. "Sorry. This is it for the day. Can they make an appointment?"

"I'm not making an appointment because you always cancel on me."

I turn at the sound of his voice and there he is, leaning on the door frame that leads to the waiting area. He's wearing all black—a leather jacket, T-shirt, and jeans with two helmets dangling from his hand.

I try to bite back my smile as I take in his hair, a rumpled, delicious mess—no doubt from the helmet— and it looks even better on him because he doesn't give a shit.

The receptionist smirks. "I'll let you work it out with him while I take care of your client at the register, but then I've gotta run. My kids have a million things going on tonight and we'll be eating dinner in the car as it is."

I turn back to my client who deserves all my attention, even if it is for just another minute. I shake out her loose curls with my fingers. "You happy?"

She beams at me through the mirror. This never gets old. "Two inches off and fresh color does a wonder for your soul. I love it. Thank you, Mary."

I unsnap her cape. "Your hubs will love it. Happy anniversary and have fun tonight."

She grabs her stuff and hurries past Evan and toward reception throwing me a grin over her shoulder. Flipping her loose waves around—she glows. "Don't worry, I'm going to have fun!"

My eyes, like magnets, wander to the man whose private parts I'm now familiar with. I've even memorized the hairline right above his beautiful cock. His whiskey eyes are hot and he looks like he'd eat me up right here if he could.

"You look at me like that much longer, you're gonna make me sorry I brought my Triumph instead of my car."

I roll my eyes before walking to the corner to grab a broom, for no other reason than I need something else to focus on besides the man who makes me forget about everything. The thought of being wrapped around Evan on a motorcycle is enough to make me fidget. This is new and, honestly, unexpected. Just a week ago, every time I saw Evan, he was either annoying me or giving me secret looks that I now know the meaning behind because they're no longer secret. He's gone from my frenemy to my lover. I know first-hand that his heated gaze packs some power—I've been the beneficiary of them over the last two days, after all.

When I turn back around to clean my station, Evan is dropping the helmets on a table and falls into my chair.

I lean on my broom and tip my head. "What are you doing?"

He puts his big biker boot to the floor and swivels the chair back and forth. "I've been secretly watching you forever and now I don't have to hide it. Do your thing. I'm just going to sit here and enjoy it."

"About that." I start to sweep the floor so I don't have to make eye contact with him. "How long?"

He stops moving and runs his boot up the back of my calf. "How long what?"

I swat his boot with the broom. "How long have you wanted me?"

"For as long as you've been avoiding me."

I stop and turn to him. "I'm serious."

"So am I. You made me work for every damn reaction I could get out of you. I was hungry for anything you'd give me. Felt like a desperate kid on the playground—thought I was going to have to pull your mermaid ponytail just to get your attention."

I cock a brow before sweeping the mess aside. "That would've pissed me off."

He's not apologetic at all when he shrugs. "I would've loved it and done it more. I can still pull your hair if you think you might be into that sort of thing."

This time I can't hide my smile and lean my thigh into the side of his where his long legs are propped on my chair. "Is that all you think about?"

"It's a lot of what I think about. What else was I supposed to do all this time you kept turning me down?"

My eyes drop to my fingers drawing patterns on his

thick thigh. "You were supposed to give up. I thought you would eventually."

He grabs my hand and twists me, pulling me into his lap. When he has my hip fit snug against his cock, he gets my full attention when he puts a hand to my chin and I have no choice but to look him in the eyes. "How many times did you turn me down when I asked you out?"

I shake my head. "Not enough apparently. You wore me down and I gave in. I already told you why I held out for so long."

"Twenty-three," he states, as serious as a stalker in any teen horror flick. And just to rub it in, he keeps on, "You turned me down twenty-three damn times. I remember every single one of them."

I glare at him. "Okay, but in my defense, I didn't think you were serious most of the time."

His hand snakes up my back and starts to play with the ends of my hair. "I'm always serious when it comes to you. You bruised my ego."

This almost makes me laugh and, given the week I've had, that's saying something. "I don't think there's one thing wrong with your ego. You're not lacking in that department."

He has the nerve to press me down into his lap. "You're right. I'm not lacking in any department."

I shake my head even though he's right.

Without warning, he changes the subject. "I talked to my dad's attorney today. The guy who's been calling you? He's on the up-and-up and has been practicing for thirty-seven years. You should call him back and see what he wants."

I shake my head. "What if it isn't good?"

He frowns. "Why do you assume it will be bad?"

My eyes widen and I roll them. "It's basically the theme of my life."

He pulls me to him and I'm forced to grab on to his wide shoulders when he puts his lips to my jaw. "Not anymore. I swear it."

I close my eyes and sink into him. "You seem really sure about everything."

He pushes me away far enough to look me in the eyes. "I am. And now that I've got you, I'm not letting anything come between us. Now, are you ready to go? I'll take you to dinner. We can stay at my place."

I look at Mr. Presumptuous but I can't make myself give him shit about anything. Not anymore. Instead, I admit what I've wanted to do now for longer than I can remember as I reach up and finger the longish hair on top of his head. "I want to cut your hair."

He tips his head. "Short?"

"No way. I'll trim it but, really, I've been itching to play with it."

A sexy smile takes over his face. "I knew you were into me."

I don't tell him how right he is. He knows. Instead, I lean in and kiss Evan Charles Hargrove III, my all-American man who I never in a million years dreamed I'd fit with, yet, here I am.

Happy.

12

IMPLODE

Evan

"GRANDPARENTS?"

Mary is sitting cross-legged next to me in my bed that's a mess from both last night and this morning's activities. She doesn't have clients until later today and, after I told Addy what was going on with Mary, she said she'd cover for me in the tasting room until we figured out this thing with Mary's dad. She did this while smiling big and told me the more time I spent with Mary, the better, and to consider it paid time off. When I asked her how much time she was spending with her new neighbor, Crew Vega, her smile turned into a glare and she told me to go home.

I told Mary to call the persistent attorney. She tried to distract me by crawling up my body, but I told her we needed to get it done and then she could use and abuse me any way she wanted.

But when she utters the word *grandparents*, her eyes go

glassy and I sit up and take her Diet Coke out of her hand so she doesn't spill it.

"I didn't know I had grandparents." She chokes on her words, her voice hoarse as she speaks into the phone. "I mean, obviously, I knew I had to have grandparents. I just figured they'd be as worthless as my mother or long dead."

I slide my hand up the outside of her bare thigh and give her a squeeze. It kills me when she looks up and a tear falls down her pale cheek.

She swallows hard and asks, "If they didn't know I existed, how did you find out about me?"

Nodding, she never takes her eyes off mine as she learns about the family she didn't know she had. After all she's told me in the last few days about her childhood, I can't imagine how she's feeling.

She rattles off her address and email, explaining that she'll get back with him, says goodbye, and drops the phone to her lap.

"You have grandparents?" I ask, hoping she's happy about the fact she has family she didn't know about.

But Mary surprises me and shakes her head. "No."

I frown and my grip on her leg tightens. "No? But I thought you said—"

She shakes her head and another tear streaks her face. "They're dead."

"Dead? Mary, tell me. What did he say?"

She swallows hard and fists my T-shirt she's wearing that's covering nothing but her bare, beautiful body. "He said they were estranged from their daughter—my mother. That she had drug problems since she was a teen and did everything they could to help her get clean, but she disappeared from their lives when she was just nineteen. They didn't know about me, at least that's what the attorney said. He had to dig to find their closest living relative and that's when he found my birth certificate. He said it wasn't easy, but he traced me from there."

"But, they're dead?"

She tries to control her emotions and shrugs. "I guess my mom's mom died years ago and the man who was my grandfather died of cancer a few weeks ago. They lived in a small town outside of Lexington."

I set my coffee down next to her Diet so I can pull her into my arms. "Baby, I'm sorry."

Her words don't match her tone—choked and shallow. "It doesn't matter. I didn't know them."

I turn my face into the side of her hair. "It does matter."

She wraps herself around me tighter. "No, it doesn't."

My neck turns wet from her tears, proof it matters a whole fucking lot.

It cuts me deep. And now I realize, feeling her cry in my arms, that from here on out, I'll do everything I can to protect her from heartache. "Tell me what else he said."

She hiccups her words. "He said he has paperwork I need to fill out. He's settling their estate and I'm their closest living relative. Because the last time they updated their wills, everything was to go to my mom and since she's dead, I guess it's mine."

"Okay, baby. I'll help you through it."

"I don't care about any of it," she keeps on through her tears and I hold her tight. "All those years ... I had grand-parents. He said they were good people—heartbroken and never the same after losing their only daughter. How could they have not known about me? How could the state not have looked harder and found them instead of putting me in foster care?"

I stroke her hair and back but don't say anything because there's nothing I can say that will make her feel better. Not after all I've learned. Nothing will take away the years she had to survive in the system. It's not lost on me that my mom got clean when I was around the same age she was when her horrors started.

I scoot down the bed and settle us on our sides, her front pressed to mine. "It's over. I'll make sure whatever you have to do is as painless as possible and we'll move on. You're not alone—not anymore and never again."

She stops talking and, even though we slept most of the night, her normal vibrant energy is zapped right out of her.

We lie like this for another hour until we're forced to get up and face the world.

Little did we know, it was about to implode.

13

ROT IN HELL

Mary

HOW MANY WAYS can another soul rock your world?

The feeling is nothing short of bizarre and I'm not sure I'll ever get used to it. I hope I don't. For as long as this lasts, I hope it feels like this each and every time he looks at me, touches me, makes me feel like I'm the only person in the universe and there's nothing on earth he'd rather be doing than focusing on me.

Me.

He spent the whole day with me at work even though I told him there was no need. He watched me and talked with my clients like they weren't just my friends, but his too. He wooed Mrs. Reichenberg, an elderly client who was in for her weekly wash and set. She was as serious as a hip-break when she told him he needed "a good, old fashioned haircut" and proceeded to boss me on what that should be. But, I swear, Evan made her blush when he explained to her that, as beautiful as she is, he's not on the market and she needed to quit hitting on him because he didn't want me to get jealous. He then gave me a heated look and told me he'll gladly surrender his beautiful locks to me to do with what I want.

Wetness instantly pooled between my legs at the thought of scheduling Evan for a private appointment.

He brought me a late lunch and a monster Diet Coke.

He played checkers with another client's five-year-old daughter because her babysitter canceled and, as all women know, World War III would have to break out before a woman would be willing to cancel a hair appointment.

He even scheduled a private wine tasting for my last appointment with all her friends at the winery, but made sure to do it on a night when I work late so he doesn't miss any time with me.

Evan didn't need to do any of this. We haven't seen or heard anything more from my dad. I don't need a babysitter and would have been fine at work with other people and he knows this. It was unspoken, but he stayed with me today because of the news I learned this morning while sitting in his bed—that I had grandparents and my childhood could've been a whole lot different.

It *should have* been different. No child should be subjected to the horrors of a broken system like I was.

Since Evan pushed his way into my life, my world continues to shift because of him.

I smile to myself on a day I never would have otherwise as I follow Evan where he's driving ahead of me in his car.

"I've got a surprise for you, little dandelion," he says over the phone.

"Everything you do is a surprise."

After work, I convinced him I needed my car so he didn't have to get up and taxi me around tomorrow. He only agreed if I promised to follow. "Is that good or bad?"

I'm quick to answer. "Good. All good. What are we doing?"

He turns west and doesn't give me any more information. "As long as the weather holds off, we'll be fine."

It's late and the sun has set. When he turns onto the road that leads to my best friend's farmhouse and business, I ask, "We're going to Addy's?"

"Not really. I'm taking you out into the vines. I don't have any tequila but do you think you can handle a glass or two of wine?"

My hangover of the decade has long come and gone and my mouth waters at the same time my stomach growls. Our late lunch was many hours ago. "As long as you feed me, too. I'm starving."

"We'll raid the kitchen first. I told Addy we were coming."

My phone beeps and I pull it away from my ear to see who it is. "Hey, I've gotta go. Piper is calling. I texted her earlier about my grandparents. I'm sure she wants to know everything. I'm right behind you."

"Okay, baby. See you in five."

I flip over to Piper's call. "Hey, you."

She doesn't bother with any greeting. "Holy shit! I want to know everything. Do you know if you have any other family?"

My insides clench because my mind hadn't gone there.

"I don't know. My mom was an only child, but I guess that doesn't mean there might not be extended family."

"I'm so sorry you're dealing with this by yourself. I wish I was there with you. I'll talk to Jake. We need to make a trip. Maybe a long weekend. I'll check on flights."

"Really?" I start to tear up at the thought of her coming to see me. Shit. There's seriously something wrong with me—I'm one Hallmark movie away from turning into a sap. I'm losing my edge I've worked so hard on all these years. I swallow over the lump in my throat and turn to follow Evan. "I would love that so much. But I'm not dealing with it alone. I was with Evan when I found out this morning."

"You were?" I hear the smile in her voice. "So, it's serious? I really like him. Whenever I text him, he gets back to me right away."

I try not to laugh because that's so Piper. "Why are you texting him?"

"To check on you." She doesn't sound the least bit repentant for her intrusion. "Because you don't text me back right away. I'm surprised you answered this call."

I shake my head. "I'm glad you feel well-informed."

"I need to meet him in person so I can make my final approval. Since I play the part of your mother, your sister, your best friend, and your—"

Oomph.

My body flies forward and the burning on the side of my face is immediate. My car swerves when something hits me from behind again.

When my brain finally clicks, I drop my phone to bring my hand to my face when my car thrashes, but not before it's angled off the dark road, jolting and bumping, until it jerks to a hard stop in the ditch.

My head pounds in a whole new way that makes my hangover feel like a papercut. Moaning, I lean back on my headrest and feel pain shoot down my neck.

The airbag in front of me deflates and I bring my trembling hand to my temple, wetness leaking down my face. When I pull my hand away, there's blood covering my fingers—I see it through the smoke. My stomach turns and, over the hiss of my engine, I hear voices in the night.

Evan

I HIT MY brakes as hard as I can when I see her headlights veer and lurch to the right in my rearview mirror.

Then, they disappear into the ditch.

"Fuck!"

I don't even bother pulling over. Throwing my car in park in the middle of the road, I swing my door open and start for the grass where Mary's car is steaming, wedged into a bank. But I hear it before I see it.

Through the dark night, there's a car. No headlights, I barely make out the shine off the windshield until the sky comes alive, lighting up the night.

Two strikes in a row, followed by booming thunder, and I see it—a dark sedan, the front of the car is smashed to shit from where it rammed Mary and pushed her off the road. The engine revs one more time but it's weak and doesn't sound like it's going anywhere. I glance to where Mary is still sitting in her car. She isn't moving.

I need to get to her so I run toward the ditch, reaching for my phone as someone gets out of the car.

"Don't move!" The drawl mixed with a rasp of cigarettes cuts through the night. "You take one step to her, I'll put a fucking bullet through your head."

I hold my hands out low. "I need to check her. She's not moving."

The man starts for me and I move in kind toward Mary. He's crazy if he thinks I'm gonna be a sitting duck. We're right outside of Addy's property. I need to get to Mary, call for help, and, somehow, I need to do that without this jackass putting a bullet in either one of us.

"I said don't move!" he booms, but the heavens argue and, when the sky lights up again, I see him.

He might be five-eight, five-nine. I have at least three inches on him. From everything she told me about him, he has aged beyond his years, but I guess prison will do that to you.

"Duane?" I call out as the rain starts. I need to go to her, call for help because if she isn't moving at this point, she's surely hurt and that kills me. But the gun dangling from his hand isn't giving me a choice and I can't turn my back on him. "I don't know what you think you want with Mary, but you're not touching her. You'll have to kill me first."

He tsks me and shakes his head. "Isn't this sweet? My little girl hooked a pretty-boy. I don't blame you, not if her snatch is as sweet as her mama's was. To this day, I've never had better. Wish she coulda handled her crank better. She brought top dollar back in the day and I got to enjoy her whenever I wanted."

Fuck. Nothing Mary told me could've lived up to this, could've prepared me for the piece of shit who gave her life. I lift my hand to pull it through my hair and his hand holding the gun jerks at my movement. I hold my ground as the rain starts to soak us to the bone. "What do you want?"

He stops about ten feet from me. The rain is pelting down and I have to squint to keep the water out of my eyes. "I know Mary's got some money comin' to her. They came to me lookin' for her. I just got out, haven't built my business up again, and I need Mary to take care of her old man. I have to do what I have to do. She won't take my calls and I've been watchin' her for a day or so. You won't leave her side so now I've gotta get through you to get to her. All I want is what Mary's mama's old man left her. It should come to me, anyway. She was my wife. Then I'll be gone for good."

"Right," I seethe, knowing for a fact Mary told me they weren't married, not that it matters anyway. I don't take my eyes off his, watching his every move, his every reaction to me. "I'm sure you'll leave her be. Until you blow it all. You and I just met, but I can tell—with your winning personality—you're probably not going to leave her to live her life in peace."

I hear a cry from the ditch and it's all I can do to hold my ground and not go to her.

The asshole starts to move to Mary. There's no way he's gonna lay a finger on her. Not while I'm still breathing.

Mary

No, not Evan.

My fucking father. He can have whatever he wants,

but I can't let anything happen to Evan. Not like this, not for me.

"You can have whatever you want." I don't even know if they can hear me through the rain.

The pain in my neck is excruciating and I think my temple is still bleeding. I do my best to reach for my seatbelt and finally unlatch it. Thunder and lightning come down around us, the heavens angry and punishing. My body screams, the hurt shooting down my back, but I twist and push my door open. Through the assaulting streams from the sky, I see them—Evan standing sentry between me and my father.

My father looks older and even harsher than I remember. I always complained about the foster homes I bounced around in like a pinball, but maybe I should be thankful he never wanted me. I'm not sure if I would've survived life with him.

"Mary, stay where you are." Evan doesn't give me a glance but his words are firm.

I look to my father and realize I'm crying. "I'll give you what you want, I promise. Just let us be."

But my heart races when he doesn't look at me. He never takes his eyes off Evan and sneers, "Trust me, boy, she's not worth it. There's too many women out there to hang it up for one, especially her."

"Evan, stop!" I beg but it's too late. When the boom fills the night again, it's a strike from heaven mingling with the one straight from hell.

Evan

I'VE HAD ENOUGH.

He raises his arm, but I've played lacrosse since I was eight. I even walked on in college and still play for recreation. Duane Giesen isn't just an asshole but a stupid one. He's underestimating me just because he's the one with a gun.

But I'm fast.

And it's fucking dark and raining.

By the time he raises his gun, I'm on the move and drop to the cold, hard, slick pavement.

Mary's screams pierce my soul at the same moment my feet get close enough to kick his out from under him. He falls with a humph and I scramble, moving for his hand. He struggles and I lunge, slamming my elbow in his throat but we're soaked to the bone and my hand slips from his forearm as he scuffles below me.

I put my weight to his chest and fight his arm as he stares up at me with a look so malicious, it sends chills down my spine. His hand starts to shake as we fight for control of the gun. "She's a piece of trash just like her mama. Not worth your life, boy."

I look into his eyes. They're shaped like Mary's, but instead of blue and bright as a perfect summer day, they're dark and evil and I'll do everything in my power to make sure they never aim their way at Mary again.

Unlike his voice that was as shaky as his weak arm, mine comes out even and I mean it with everything I am. "Rot in hell."

Mary

THEY'RE ROLLING ON the ground and my father has already shot at him once.

"Stop!" I try but it's useless. My voice is weak and, when I push myself to my feet in the muddy ditch where my car landed, my head spins. I take one step toward them and lose my footing. I fall and the stormy night gets gloomier until my vision spirals into nothing and, as my ears ring and I fall into blackness, the last thing I hear is a second gunshot...

Evan

FEET HIT PAVEMENT—AND not just one pair. I'm not sure how I hear it through the storm, but the closer they get, the faster they are, splashing water with every stomp.

I fall back to my ass and watch the blood seep out of Mary's father faster than what seems natural because of the puddle he's lying in.

"Evan?"

I jerk and look up, my lungs searching for air.

It's not the first time in my life I've shot a gun, but I drop it to the pavement next to me as Addy's new neighbor, Crew Vega, and another man come running up to me. I've only met Crew a few times and he's seemed cool, but I just shot a man and I need to get to Mary.

"I..." I try to catch my breath.

"Don't say anything," the older one directs. "We saw it all go down on the cameras. Tried to get to you as fast as we could. We've got a car coming."

I look up at them through the rain. "Cameras?"

Crew holds out a hand to me but weirdly says, "Go

check on Mary. Make sure she's stable. At this point, Grady will be able to get her to the hospital faster than waiting for an ambulance. Asa and I'll clean this up."

I have no idea who Grady or Asa are but, right now, I don't give a shit. I scramble to my feet and run the ten yards to where Mary is lying in the wet grass, rain coming down on her fair skin that's now paler than normal. I fall to my knees and feel her pulse, strumming below her skin. I have no idea if it's fast or slow or normal, but it's there.

I put my hand to her face and brush her cheek. "Baby. Wake up. Mary, please."

Her eyes flutter and she murmurs, "Dizzy. So dizzy."

"You're going to be okay. It's all over." I don't know if it's a lie, but right now I'll will it to be true. I let out a breath and pull her off the cold, wet ground and into my arms.

One of the men crouches next to us and looks into her eyes with the flashlight on his phone, making her wince. "I'm one of Crew's men. Name's Asa. She's got a pretty big knot on her head—could have a concussion. Careful with her neck. You need help getting her up or are you good?"

I pull her into my arms—because there's no way I'm letting her go—and stand. "I'm good."

When we climb to the road, a black Escalade appears, the headlights lighting up the night. Crew opens the back door and motions for me to get in. "Grady will drive you to the hospital. It was a hit-and-run—Mary slid off the road. You got me, Evan?"

I climb into the back of the SUV, only thinking of Mary, and try to put everything else out of my head.

"Evan, Grady will explain more on the way, but tell me you get it," Crew directs one more time.

I give him a chin lift and look down at Mary tucked to my chest. "Yeah."

With that, Crew slams my door.

And today is the day I realize, you might think you know someone, but in reality, you have no fucking clue.

14

I KNOW YOU

Mary

"BABY, HERE'S YOUR coffee."

That's a new voice. Besides Evan, Addy, Bev, the nurses, and an occasional doctor, no one else has been here. That deep gravelly tone is one I've never heard before.

"Thank you. I don't care what her vitals say, I'm not moving from this chair until I see for myself that she's okay."

Even though my aching body protests, I know that voice. I turn to the sweet sound that feels like home. Prying my eyes open, I have to squint because of the light. I hate that my voice is weak and laced with emotion from seeing my best friend for the first time in way too long. "You're really here?"

Piper doesn't take her eyes off me as she pushes her Starbucks to-go cup toward a huge man and stands from the chair, rushing to my side. "Thank God. It didn't matter how many times they told me you'd be okay. There's nothing like seeing your bright blue eyes."

I try to return her squeeze since she's taken my good hand, but I'm so tired. "You read my chart? How do you know what it means? I'm not a cupcake recipe."

My beautiful friend smiles and her eyes turn glassy.

I try to clear my dry throat. "How did you get here?"

Piper swipes a quiet tear running down her cheek and reaches for a water cup on the table, offering me the straw. "I freaked out after I heard you scream on the phone right before the line went dead. I blew up Evan's phone until he called me last night and told me everything about the hit and run. You're lucky it wasn't worse—your car could've rolled in that storm. I lost it and Jake booked flights for first thing this morning. We came straight to the hospital and I've been waiting on you to wake up."

A man I recognize only from pictures walks up behind Piper and leans down to press his lips to the top of her head. I wasn't able to travel back to be at their wedding. "I'm Jake Hyde. Good to see you awake. Not quite sure I've ever seen anything put my wife in such a state and knew I had to get her here as soon as I could."

I take in my best friend and her new husband as I try to muster my best post-concussion, cracked-ribs, broken-wrist smile. "Thank you."

I look around the room and realize he's not here.

I came-to in his arms last night in a strange car on the way to the emergency room. Evan explained it was over and Addy's neighbor would take care of everything with the hit and run. Even with a throbbing head, an aching arm, and my body protesting every bump and turn the SUV was making, I saw it in his eyes.

And I knew.

So, when the police questioned me late last night, I took Evan's lead and told them the truth—that a car hit me from behind and I passed out. With Evan sitting next to me, he gave my hand a squeeze and explained the rest. That it was my father and he had an altercation with him to keep him from getting to me.

The truth.

Ish.

Now, there's a warrant out for Duane Giesen's arrest for hit and run along with assault.

There are only five of us who know that warrant will stay outstanding. Forever.

Now, for the first time since we got to the emergency room last night, Evan isn't by my side.

"He stepped out to talk with a man who came to check on you. I think his name is Crew? They didn't want to wake you," Piper explains, knowing I'm looking for Evan before I have a chance to ask. "He said he was Addy's neighbor. I can't wait to meet her. He said she'd be by soon to bring you lunch so you wouldn't have to eat hospital food."

I swallow and nod, my head swimming and not only from my concussion.

"I hope you know," Piper adds, "I was all ready to pack you up and move you home with us. I wasn't even going to let you argue. But we've been here for less than two hours and I can already see how many people you have who love you."

"Yeah," I agree and let that sink deep into my heart that's softening to the idea more and more that I actually have people and they might just love me as much as I do them.

Evan

"MARY DOESN'T HAVE anything to worry about when it comes to her dad," Crew explains in a low voice. "And neither do you."

I drop my head to look at my feet as I rub the tense muscles on the back of my neck. Exhaling, I release the stress I've been hoarding since last night. I know Mary won't ever have to worry about her dad. I was the one who made sure of that. But I have to know, so I look to the man I've only met a handful of times at Addy's who clearly has an interest in my boss. "Why?"

He doesn't move—his body in a weird state of wired yet relaxed. "Why what?"

"Why did you do it?"

He doesn't flinch but answers, knowing exactly what I mean. "Because it was the right thing to do and, I don't care how ugly shit might get, I always go with my gut."

I look to my side and I'm not sure I can accept that as an answer. Not after last night—whatever the hell happened after we left the scene. Not after Grady explained how it would go down on the way to the hospital and, even though I didn't have time to ask why, there was something about him, Asa, and Crew that made me go along with everything. And there's the fact I wasn't excited to explain to the police I killed a man, even though it was in self-defense.

Or, mostly in self-defense which was why I had no problem agreeing.

Folding my arms across my chest, I keep on because I have to know. "You don't know me."

"I do." Crew's answer comes quick. "Almost as well as you know yourself. I know Bev, Morris, Van, and Maggie. I even know Clara's kids are a pain in the ass. Addy's mine and that means I know everything about everyone in her life. You were a rowdy kid—but a good one—who's become an even better man. And I know the woman lying in that hospital bed needs you. Hell, she needs everyone, just as much as Addy needs me—she just hasn't figured it out yet. So, yeah, Evan. I know you."

All I can do is stare at him and ask, "But I don't know you."

"You know enough. I got your back. So do my men. That's all you need to know."

I take in a deep breath. "Fuck."

Crew doesn't say another word but the sides of his lips tip and he gives me a shrug.

He's right. Not only do I not need to know anything else, I don't want to.

"Tell Mary I hope she feels better soon. I'm sure I'll catch up with her at Addy's." With that, Crew turns and walks down the hall as if he's not a guy who knows how to get rid of a dead body and cover up a murder—albeit justified.

Shifting, I turn the handle to Mary's door and hear Piper talking nonsense about Mary moving back to Massachusetts.

"The only place Mary is moving is in with me."

Mary turns, her bright blue eyes finding mine. Blue eyes that may be tired, worn down, and bloodshot, but one thing they aren't, is scared. And I'm the one who made sure of that.

I'll never question Crew or his men again.

"I missed you," she admits freely.

I go straight to her and put my lips to hers. "I was only gone for three minutes. Crew said to tell you to feel better and he'd see you at Addy's."

She nods and doesn't give Crew a second thought. "So, I'm moving in with you?"

"Addy and Bev are moving some of your things to my condo now. We can get the rest later when you're feeling up to it."

She threads her fingers through mine and tips her head toward me on her pillow. "I guess you've got everything under control then, huh?"

"You don't have to worry about anything ever again, baby." I give her hand a squeeze and I see relief in her eyes. "I promise."

"I'm worried her dad will be back. He's already proved how desperate he is," Piper says.

I glance at Piper, shake my head, and tell her the truth. "Mary will be with me and I have a feeling after last night, we've seen the last of him. When I looked into his eyes the last time, he was scared shitless."

"I hope you're right." Piper sighs before her gaze settles on Mary. "Guess what? Jake and I are staying on Evan's family farm—in a guest house!"

Mary smiles at her friend before throwing me a glance, no doubt her thoughts mirroring mine. I rub my jaw and wet my lip just thinking about our time there and make a mental note to take her back as soon as she's feeling up to it.

She looks back to Piper. "You're going to love it. And there are horses—even a colt. Maybe you can whip up a recipe to bake them organic treats."

I watch Mary talk and smile and try not to laugh so she doesn't hurt her ribs as she catches up with her best friend. I get to know Jake Hyde and learn about his business.

After all this time of me wanting Mary, I had no clue just how badly the thought of losing her would hurt.

And I vow to myself, that will never happen again.

EPILOGUE

My Dandelion

Mary
Two months later.

E VAN AND I have settled into our new normal. I've officially moved into his condo and let my crappy apartment go. Something that couldn't have come at a better time with cracked ribs and a broken wrist.

My grandparents' estate was just settled last week. I've been spending all my extra time looking through photos, getting to know the family I didn't know I had. Besides names and dates, there is very little to learn. I did find out that I have extended family scattered around, but I haven't had the nerve to reach out to them yet. Evan told me there's no hurry and, when or if I felt like it, he'll be by my side.

I don't question that. He hasn't budged an inch from my side and I couldn't be happier about it.

I spent my life itching to turn eighteen so I could be on my own and, since then, have lived in the moment. I haven't thought about the future in years but, in the last few weeks, I've allowed myself to ... *dream.*

Not plan. Don't get crazy, I'm not to that level of adulting yet. Maybe someday, but not today.

But the more I allow myself to dream, the further those dreams wander. They've gone as far as a wedding, a home, a family...

It's still hard for me to make plans for the future but one thing in those dreams is a constant—Evan is in every single one of them. It's settling into my soul that he's a reality.

"Mom." Evan sighs as he plays with the ends of my hair, his arm resting on the back of my chair. "Give it a rest with the questions."

I reach with my hand and give his thigh a squeeze and realize how good it feels to do that. I got the cast off my arm last week. "It's okay."

"See, sweetheart? She said it's fine." Nina raises a brow at her son before looking back at me with a kind smile. "We want to know everything about you."

Evan gives my hair a tug. "She's in girlfriend heaven. I can't stop her."

I settle into the crook of his arm and finally relax. This is my first time meeting Evan's parents and to say I was nervous is an understatement. They've been home from Europe for two weeks and Evan dragged his feet until I got the cast off my arm. I wanted to start my new life off fresh, no reminders of anything that had to do with my father. Evan gave me that.

He also must have prepared his parents for all that is me because so far Nina Hargrove has asked me a million questions but not one of them has had to do with my family, childhood, or basically anything prior to my eighteenth birthday. As we sit on their massive patio next to the outdoor wood-burning fireplace that's crackling away to cut the autumn chill while we have dinner, I've answered questions about my career in cosmetology, my short-lived time in college, and my friendship with Addy Wentworth.

Evan Charles Hargrove Jr. and his wife are kind and genuine. Even though I can't say I know any multi-gazillionaires, they aren't what I expected. Evan is very much like them yet, still, he couldn't be more different. On the outside, his parents look like they belong at Churchill Downs but they don't act like it. I do secretly wonder how many hats his mother owns. It's plain to see they love Evan and, even though theirs isn't a big family, it's the same love I felt every time I was at Piper's with she and her dad.

I return Nina's smile. "It's really okay."

Evan's dad finishes off his dessert and wipes his mouth before clearing his throat. "Nina's just excited. We've never seen our son like this before. From all he's said and now seeing the two of you together, I wouldn't be surprised if he'd walk through fire and take on the world for you."

I look at their son, who I've fallen completely and madly in love with, to find his eyes burning into me. The same eyes that hold not only my heart, but all my secrets.

I'm pretty sure my heart skips a beat like it always does when Evan looks at me like this. He doesn't have to say it, although he does multiple times every day.

He loves me.

And, yes, his dad is right. But he's also wrong. Evan doesn't need to take on the world for me.

He already has.

And he won. There's nothing left to do but for me to try to love him back—to try to give him a fraction of what he gives me.

I'm not sure what kind of prize I am. My dad selling my mom for sex while keeping her strung out isn't exactly goal-worthy.

To this day, I wonder what I did to deserve Evan. I'll probably never stop wondering, even though a couple weeks ago I told him I loved him and I've never loved anyone in my life.

I already knew he loved me. He whispered it into my ear on the way to the hospital that night while he was begging me to open my eyes. It was the best way to regain consciousness.

Evan leans in and puts his lips to my now fully-healed temple. "She's worth it."

I'd argue or chastise him for kissing me in front of his parents when I already warned him on the way here not to, but I don't get a chance to do either because I hear a sniffle from across the table as Nina breaks into the moment.

When we look at her, she's dabbing her eyes and Evan groans. "Mom."

"Sorry." She waves us off. "I'm just happy to be here to see this."

A comment like that coming from his mom who has faced her own demons means something—it isn't some throw-away remark.

Life. It's as delicate and beautiful as a lily but some-times to survive it, you have to be strong.

Like a dandelion.

Evan

Six Years later.

"Would you like to bang the gavel?"

I look down at my seven-year-old daughter as my two-year-old son wiggles in my arms, with my six-month pregnant wife standing next to me as she wipes a tear from her fair cheek.

We've come a long way since that night she drank too much tequila at an Italian restaurant.

Thirty seconds ago, I wasn't a dad. Not officially.

But I sort of was the day the Commonwealth of Virginia placed Cora and Caleb with us sixteen months ago. Caleb doesn't remember a time when our large country home wasn't his.

Cora does. She was five-and-a-half and, I'm not gonna lie, the first six months were rough.

But Mary knew exactly what Cora needed and I followed her lead.

Their biological father is dead and their birth mom has given up all rights. She hasn't seen them since the day the Commonwealth rescued them from the Godforsaken apartment where they were found, dirty and hungry. They were brought to us in the middle of the night a week after we were cleared to become foster parents and, the moment I learned their story, I knew.

No, the moment I saw Mary lay eyes on them, that's when I had no doubt.

They'd be ours someday.

That someday is officially today.

Cora grabbing that gavel, using all her might to bang the shit out of the wooden block, seals it. But she misses, dents the judge's desk, and the packed room erupts.

Cora looks up to Mary in horror but my wife runs her fingers through Cora's dark wavy hair. "It's okay, baby."

The judge even laughs. "Every time I look at that, I'm going to think of you and smile, Cora Hargrove."

Cora looks up at the judge. "It's finally real?"

The judge sticks out his hand. "Congratulations on your new mom and dad."

Shit, we need to work on her hand-shaking etiquette because Cora blows him off, turns to jump into Mary's arms, and squeals.

Mary sheds more tears.

Piper leaves Jake's side and wraps her arms around my wife and daughter.

My mom plucks Caleb from my arms and he goes to his grandparents as if he's known them every moment he's been on this earth.

Addy, Maya, Keelie, and Gracie go straight to Mary.

I turn to find Crew, Grady, Asa, and Jarvis standing there with their families. Crew offers me his hand and, when I take it, he lowers his voice. "Knew it'd be worth it."

I haven't spoken a word about that night since Crew disappeared down the hospital corridor the day after I put a bullet through Duane Giesen's head. I don't say anything but nod as Grady slaps me on the back. "Talk about jumping into the fire. Congratulations, man."

I'm about to thank him but I feel her. I turn to my wife and she comes up on her toes. I meet her as I dip my hand into her hair that's now all blond and put my mouth to hers.

"Thank you," she whispers for only me to hear. "You've made our lives beautiful today and I love you for it. Thank you for wanting my dream as much as me."

With a tug at my arm, I let Mary go long enough to pick up Cora.

As our daughter giggles, our son belly laughs while my dad hangs him upside down by his feet, and our family and friends surround us, I feel our youngest kick from inside Mary's belly as she's pressed up next to me.

Life is never what you expect.

I look down at my wife. "I'll do anything for you, baby. Anything."

She knows and nods.

Strong, beautiful, a survivor.

My dandelion.

Thank you for reading. If you enjoyed *The Tequila*, I would appreciate a review on Amazon.

Read Crew and Addy's story in *Vines*
Read Grady and Maya's story in *Paths*
Read Asa and Keelie's story in *Gifts*
Read Jarvis and Gracie's story in *Veils*
Read Cole and Bella's story in *Scars*
Read Ozzy and Liyah's story in *Souls*

The Next Generation
Read *Levi*, Asa's son

ACKNOWLEDGMENTS

THANK YOU TO my family—the Mister, my three kids, my perfect dog, and even my lizard, thank you for your love, patience, and support as I chase my dreams.

Elle—you and your family inspired this story. I love you like a sister and miss you every day.

Kristan—you continue to polish and pretty up my words like an artist. Thank you for working alongside me and putting up with all my chapter thirteens.

To my betas—Ivy, Laurie, and Gi, your time and investment in me is a gift and I adore you all. Kolleen, Carrie, Ashley, Penny, Gillian, Pat, Janet, Michelle, and Annette, I don't know what I would do without every single one of you. Thank you for your help and wanting my books to be everything I do.

Layla and Sarah—your friendship means the world. Thank you for sharing the trivial parts of my very boring life … daily. Hourly. Okay, fine, whatever—by the minute.

Finally, and most importantly, I wouldn't be doing this without my readers and ARC team. Thank you loving my characters, wanting my stories, and pushing me to give you the books you want. I do it all for you.

ALSO BY BRYNNE ASHER

Killers Series

Vines – A Killers Novel, Book 1

Paths – A Killers Novel, Book 2

Gifts – A Killers Novel, Book 3

Veils – A Killers Novel, Book 4

Scars – A Killers Novel, Book 5

Souls – A Killers Novel, Book 6

The Tequila – A Killers Novella

The Killers, The Next Generation

Levi, Asa's son

The Agents

Possession

Tapped

Exposed

Illicit

The Carpino Series

Overflow – The Carpino Series, Book 1

Beautiful Life – The Carpino Series, Book 2

Athica Lane – The Carpino Series, Book 3

Until Avery – A Carpino Series Crossover Novella

Force of Nature - A Carpino Christmas Novel

The Dillon Sisters

Deathly by Brynne Asher

Damaged by Layla Frost

The Montgomery Series

Bad Situation – The Montgomery Series, Book 1

Broken Halo – The Montgomery Series, Book 2

Betrayed Love - The Montgomery Series, Book 3

Standalones

Blackburn

ABOUT THE AUTHOR

Brynne Asher lives in the Midwest with her husband, three children, and her perfect dog. When she isn't creating pretend people and relationships in her head, she's running her kids around and doing laundry. She enjoys cooking, decorating, shopping at outlet malls and online, always seeking the best deal. A perfect day in Brynne World ends in front of an outdoor fire with family, friends, s'mores, and a delicious cocktail.

facebook.com/brynneasherauthor

instagram.com/brynneasher

amazon.com/Brynne-Asher/e/B00VRULS58/ref=dp_by-line_cont_pop_ebooks_1

bookbub.com/profile/brynne-asher

Printed in Great Britain
by Amazon